What People Are Saying About the *Pain Before the Rainbow*

"This phenomenally well-written book is the story of personal pain; seconds, minutes, days, and decades of tears, screams, hurt and ugliness, despair, and loss of hope.

This book is about the absolute bravery it takes to write and talk about what really needs to be said… Jack Cooper finds no more hiding. No more rehashing the traumas.

This book is about YOU!

Your tears will eventually dry up as you open and engulf every page; discover your gorgeous rainbow brilliance in being the most amazing you."

—Joanie Lindenmeyer
Best-Selling Author of *Nun Better: An Amazing Love Story*
Co-author with Elizabeth Ann Atkins:
Joyously Free! Stories & Tips to Live your Truth as LGBTQ+ People, Parents and Allies And *Healing Religious Hurts: Stories & Tips to Find Love and Peace*

"Cooper's perfectly flowing prose reaches that elusive place where reality and fiction—*biomythography*—collide seamlessly. His ability to infuse his characters and settings with his heartbreaking depth makes this anthology unforgettable. Both uplifting and somber, Cooper's heart and humanity reflect the wisdom of his journey."

—Glenn E. Kakely, LCSW
Author of *The Power to Create You*

"A time before the rainbow was a period in America when the vileness of those who didn't understand the humanity of the LGBTQ+ community was immeasurable. Today, given the current political environment, it appears to be a *here we go again moment*. Cooper's *Pain Before the Rainbow* is timely as it is historical… implications of loss and time and what it means to be haunted by both. Cooper's biomythography is a reminder not to allow a return to the time before the rainbow."

—Laureen R. Violante, CMT, CYT
certified meditation and yoga teacher
and co-founder of YogaTales

"These stories explore enduring glimmers of compassion, hope, love, and kindness in the shadow of a purity culture and the Church's darkness. Your heart will bleed—maybe for the first time—and it should."

—James Buono
Family Trauma and Loss Counselor

"In *Anthony's Sin*, Jack Cooper takes us into the minds and hearts of two young men as they discover beautiful passion while grappling with poignant pain inflicted by a world that does not yet accept or celebrate love outside its rigid hetero norms. Hence, the fitting title of this brilliant collection, *Pain Before the Rainbow*.

It's important to read this novella that takes place only a few short decades ago, before the rainbow helped cultivate and sustain today's freedoms. Cooper's powerful stories help us remember and reflect on the pain of the past, before same-sex marriage was legal, before Pride month marches electrified cities around the world, and before LGBTQ+ people were included and celebrated in the media and mainstream society.

While his stories show how bad it once was, they renew our commitment to never allowing the world to slip backwards. Courageous and insightful writers like Cooper help us move forward with respect, love, and harmony for all."

—Elizabeth Ann Atkins
Co-Founder
Two Sisters Writing & Publishing®

Pain Before the Rainbow:

a biomythographical anthology

Anthony's Sin and Other Stories

by Jack Cooper

Pain Before the Rainbow: a biomythographical anthology
Anthony's Sin and Other Stories
Copyright © 2025 Jack Cooper
All Rights Reserved.

No part of this publication may be reproduced, stored in
a retrieval system or transmitted, in any form or by any
means—electronic, mechanical, photocopying, recording,
or otherwise—without prior written permission from the
publisher, except for the inclusion of brief quotations in a review.

For information about this title or to order other books
and/or electronic media, contact the publisher:

Two Sisters Writing & Publishing®
TwoSistersWriting.com
18530 Mack Avenue, Suite 166
Grosse Pointe Farms, MI 48236

Paperback ISBN: 978-1-956879-82-7
Ebook ISBN: 978-1-956879-83-4

Printed in the United States of America.

Book cover design and interior formatting: Van-garde Imagery, Inc.

Author photo: Jack Cooper's Photo Collection.

Dedication

For Glenn, my friend, lover, soul mate, and husband, for his understanding and support, and whose compassion encouraged my journey of healing and growth.

And to all those whose journeys ended prematurely either by their own hands or by those who never fully understood or accepted us during a time before the rainbow.

I have written about my experiences of love and tragic death. My purpose was to allow this to heal me, not to entertain you—I've given no thought to serving you or my reputation. I couldn't possibly do so. These stories were written to help me understand who I am more fully and to comprehend my own journey.

Thank you for allowing me to share this with you.

Acknowledgements

Writing is often considered a solitary endeavor, but this book is the culmination of the support, encouragement, and expertise of some remarkable individuals. I am deeply grateful for their contributions and would like to take this opportunity to acknowledge some of them.

First and foremost, I would like to extend my heartfelt thanks to my loving husband. His unwavering belief in my abilities provided the foundation upon which I built this work. To my sister, who, along with my husband and soulmate, has been my biggest cheerleader; your unwavering support and encouragement have been invaluable.

I am also profoundly grateful to my editor and publisher, Elizabeth Ann Atkins of Two Sisters Writing and Publishing®. Her keen insights and constructive feedback were not just helpful, but instrumental in shaping the manuscript into its final form. Your dedication and expertise have been crucial in refining my writing and strengthening the narrative.

Thank you to best-selling author Joanie Lindenmeyer for your enthusiasm for my work. Your continued support in championing my book will be crucial into bringing this book to the world and to the many who may benefit from its stories.

I want to express my appreciation to my past colleagues and current friends. Your love and camaraderie have been a source of inspiration throughout my life's journey. Special thanks to all my LGBTQ friends, past and present, who have touched my life in the most invaluable ways. This book is also for you.

To the many authors and writers who have influenced and inspired me, I owe a debt of gratitude. Your work has shaped my thinking and approach to storytelling.

To all of my children, who continue to give me love and affection and the reasons to go on.

Finally, I would like to extend my heartfelt appreciation to my readers. Your enthusiasm and support are not just encouraging, but make this endeavor worthwhile. I hope this book resonates with you and stimulates your compassion and tribute for those who didn't make the journey with us.

Thank you all for being part of this journey.

Table of Contents

Section III

Biomythography

Although this story is biomythographical, the names and other identifying characteristics have been changed.

> *Biomythography—weaving together myth, history, and biography in epic narrative form, a style of composition that represents all the ways in which we perceive the truth. Biomythography is not our truth simply and mundane, but a writing down of our meanings of identity... with the materials of our lives. We are the culmination of it all; experiences are painted with imagery, perception, and mostly of emotions. Details that become true in the telling.*[1]

Biomythography is a genre that was created by Black lesbian poet and author Audre Lorde with her 1982 book, *Zami: A New Spelling of My Name.* She wrote that this genre enables us to use our experiences to compose what identity means to us, and that we can use emotions, along with imagery and perception, to express our truths.[2]

Section I

Pain Before the Rainbow

I'm glad you made it. I'm glad many of us made it, as there was pain before the rainbow—deadly pain. Gay pride and the birth of the rainbow flag were a seventies phenomenon. Before the rainbow—the flag of identity, solidarity, and pride—there was the tragic loss of so many of us.

I was a teenager when, in 1978, Gilbert Baker, an American artist and gay rights activist, gave us the rainbow only several years after the events of Stonewall and the liberation and social movements that followed—the birth of Pride. Pride is essential because someone today still believes they're better off dead than being gay, especially in the South, especially the Christian.

I think of these things, and all the time, the astonishment of being a survivor weighs me down. So many of us, by our own hand, perished. Those I knew and those I did not know.

I know perfectly well that to have reached the defining years of adulthood, given who and what we were, was a triumph. I have escaped death by my own hand on more than one occasion. I have escaped death, while there were those who, given who and what they were, did not escape and are absent from my life.

To survive, I've had to create a family beyond the ties of flesh and blood, an ever-changing family of people, passing faces and smiles that have left their marks on my journey. Yes, there was pain, deadly pain, before the rainbow.

When I write of the pain, I do not only write about my youth but also the bits and pieces of me: who I am, what I've become, and who I'm perceived to be. This is my identity.

That painful part of my past has a great deal to do with who I am today. A memoir of my younger years would explain much of what has become my living history. This is how it felt to me, how I remember experiencing it emotionally, and how it has forever touched me. As much as I would like to say that I'm being faithful to how it was—those places, those people, the emotions, all the little details—this is the best I can do given the passage of time.

This is a reflection—not precisely as it was, for that would not be possible and would not be prudent. But, as a *biomythography*, I must fill in the blanks, and there are many. Filling in the blanks of my memory is necessary to help convey meaning, emotion, pain— the scars that I bear. I don't say that to elicit sympathy or identify as a victim.

This is as I felt it, as I lived it—my experiences, emotions, and the wounds that were suffered. These memories are deeply rooted in the emotional, physical, and spiritual toll that has defined me. Experiences that couldn't be expressed without writing about them. However, the words conveying these feelings are wholly inadequate, as they do not do justice to those emotions that they attempt to convey. But it is all I have to work with if I am to share them, and I must share them because this pain is like poison. It eats away from the inside.

As a young child, I knew those feelings defining who I was, what I was, and what I was to become. I knew nothing of what those feelings meant. They just were. I did not think that they were anything but natural. I only knew they were necessary for me to feel whole. At the time, it was like having a sensation of yearning for something that defied articulation. To enjoy the emotional bond with another boy was something I was awakened to long before sexuality was a conscious awareness. I cultivated boy friendships easily as if it were the natural thing to do. Real fondness for another boy was as fulfilling as anything else I knew.

As a child and over many years, I was inoculated with the belief that I was, and my feelings were, considered disturbed, immoral, a sin. That is what started the very bad days. The questions were always there, and in unexpected moments, they would muscle their way into my consciousness, positioning stubbornly at the forefront of my mind. Was I what they said I was? Was I disturbed by having the feelings that were most natural for me? Am I condemned as a sinner for my thoughts, feelings, and desires?

Yes, those were the bad days. Days when I was truly alone, struggling with those questions. Much of the pain of loneliness has to do with concealment, feeling compelled to hide vulnerability, tuck away, and cover up those natural feelings that others find ugly and repulsive. Pain gave me the right to be angry—that barbaric and undignified emotion that would mask my fear, hurt, and embarrassment.

I would retreat to my alone place for hours, contemplating the aberration that possessed me. And in that place, and during those hours, life seemed hopeless, pointless. And then the black of the night would settle upon me. I had survived another day without divulging any of my secrets. I placed another day between the person I knew I was and the person I was perceived to be. It always seemed an accomplishment worthy of sleep. So, I would close my eyes and ready myself for another day in a world that would not accept me as I was. Yet I slept well, given the emotional exhaustion that shrouded me.

Despite my desperate prayers, morning would arrive once more, finding me still alive—yet another disappointment from the God they often spoke of. The God who provided the rules. So, I would open my eyes to survive another day in a world that was not accepting of me. I did it when I felt so awful that sometimes the pain transported me to another state of mind where everything, even the feelings I worked so hard to ignore, seemed to fade into mind-numbing grief.

I did it when my hopelessness crowded out all other thoughts. It took real effort and concentration to tether myself to this life that I wanted to end as many have. It took real effort to keep myself from raging with despair and shame. I would face another day even when I was so exhausted from feeling the shame of knowing my demons were mine alone. It demanded such energy that I had to lie in bed thinking of reasons to get up and live another day when it would have been much easier to go to my alone place and surrender. Yes, those were the very bad days.

I was not living my life as much as I merely existed in it. But sometimes, that was okay, as simply living was difficult enough. Depressive episodes would close around me like a curtain and could hang on to me for weeks, months, or years.

The challenge was the need to live two lives. One was authentic and seldom lived; one was theater for those who needed me to perform within it. One was subversive—the real me, and one was dutiful—that which was expected of me. One was emotional and passionate, and one was the expectations of others. The effort required to keep one from the other and yet keep both alive was exhausting. Every day would end with complete fatigue. Yes, I slept well.

The only essential aspects of my identity were my sexual prowess in one life and professional accomplishments and money in my other life. And I was an achiever in all three, and often without honor. Eventually, one life would have to give way to the other. A fact that I often feared yet knew was inevitable. Ultimately, my carelessness and weakness brought about the unavoidable singular life. The transition was beyond horrible, a shift that took several years, if ever complete. I believed that I would not come out of it in a healthy place, if I came out of it at all, as many did not. The immense harm done to others and me during the process was unfortunate. But it's over, I believe, and I've made peace with it.

There was a time when the soul's endless yearnings had to be kept secret. The damage that has been done to the heart, the mind, and the spirit cannot be undone. The spirit can be wounded as physically as the body, and when these wounds do not heal, well… I cannot conceive of anyone at a young age during a time before the rainbow, who was not irreparably scarred knowing the conditions of this life. We were innocent bystanders, caught up in a society that dictated more than the who, what, and when of our young lives. The wonder is not that so many of us perished by our own hands, but that so many of us survived at all.

As I look back, surviving when so many others had surrendered, I question whether my coming through it should be considered a victory. The tragic loss of so many like us often negates any satisfaction of attaining my true self. What of those who didn't make it? Are they simply memories, if remembered at all? Are they remembered for who they were or who they were perceived to be, hoped to have been? Is that the *real* tragedy?

I miss those who didn't make the journey with me, even those I didn't know. But those I knew certainly left scars upon me when they departed. And the emotional attachment still survives today. It always will. I should not forget them. I will not forget them. I cannot forget the pain before the rainbow.

Yes, I am glad you made it. I am happy many of us made it.

I Was a Child When…

…I learned that there was something shameful about loving boys, especially since I was a boy. My unsavory attachment to other boys represented everything that my childhood had asked me not to be, and I didn't understand it. I was clueless about those unnamable feelings that had taken hold of me.

At the time, I hadn't yet learned that my inclinations provoked such distaste from others. I was not yet aware of the social and religious norms that suggested something weak or unhealthy about my feelings. What sort of boy craves affection from other boys? What boy could be so soft and sensitive? Such feelings were not normal. They were worse than sinful, even; they were emblematic of depravity itself. If having affection or desire for other boys was as perverse as others said it was, then what would they think about *my* affection and desire for another boy?

I was raised among Italians, all deeply Catholic. In the 1960s and 70s, America was still a Puritan country when it came to same-sex affection. Everything in a boy's education focused on making him manly. The official culture of my youth was Boy Scouting, team sports, and religious instruction. Street culture provided schoolyard fights, bullying, and neighborhood gangs. There was no escaping manhood, responsible or otherwise, without persecution and disgrace. I was an innocent bystander caught up in a society that dictated the who, what, and when of my young life.

At a certain point, I realized that I was different from the other boys. I was a boy who wanted to be with other boys. I had no interest in sports. I avoided group activities. In my working-class neighborhood, boy culture was rough and tumble and hierarchical. Most of the misbehavior was mindless anarchy. I never picked a fight, but I fought back ferociously when pushed around. I didn't need to win to demonstrate that I could be like them in appearance. But I had the distinct feeling that something about me was different in ways that weren't always visible.

I was moved and motivated by things different from those of my peers. Other kids seemed not to notice the things that moved me deeply. When I saw a boy that attracted me, it gave me more than simple pleasure; it left me breathless. I felt the sense of my existence enlarge in unaccountable ways. I wanted to stay in the enchantment. I hungered for more.

I preferred sensory and sensual phantasms to the everyday reality of my school and neighborhood life, and I learned over time that it was so shameful that I needed to keep it hidden. I couldn't put my desires into words back then, but I felt them keenly. My fantasies were not just escapist pastimes. They were abnormal passions. I was a mutant, a monster with a freakish vulnerability for other boys. Years later, I found a name for my debilitation—gay.

The exquisite pleasures my affections gave me were the first stirrings of sexual desire, but it was less specific and had no easy outlet. My desires were desperate yet enigmatic. I could not explain what I burned for, except that I wanted it more than anything. I wasn't sure what that meant.

While the other boys watched Carl Yastrzemski and Hank Aaron play ball, I watched the other boys. Same-sex attractions gave me bewildering pleasure. It would take me out of myself and into the animating presence of something I craved but did not understand. Comprehension had nothing to do with it. What mattered was being in its presence. Real life seemed small in comparison.

I wasn't seeking knowledge or wisdom. I wasn't even seeking pleasure. I wanted to surrender to an ecstasy beyond my control and understanding. Same-sex attractions left me no wiser, just happier. They took me out of my ordinary self. Yet the emotional intensity gave it a visceral credibility. I struggled to describe something invisible, intangible, and unknowable.

I wanted to share my feelings, but I knew it would be a mistake to try. It was best to hide my passions. Why add weak and weird to who I was? Many children lead secret lives. Mine was more unusual than most, as far as I knew. In public, I was an excellent student, even if I was also a loner who was terrible at sports. It was not a glamorous identity, but it was a manageable one. In private, I was a pleasure-lover who lived in his imagination, fired by same-sex mysteries. I was never bored by solitude. I was preoccupied with things I believed no one else was.

It made everyday living more difficult. I didn't understand the attraction to boys. However, I recognized that I could not cultivate this vulnerability. It needed to be suppressed. There was no one to ask for advice; I could only wait and watch. Neither I nor the world was likely to change. I formed strong opinions based on scant experience. I would find a way to lead two lives. I hoped there would eventually be someone for me to talk to, so that I could be validated someday. That validation wouldn't come for many, many years.

A Cowboy Lost

Just off the tree-lined campus of our eastside high school was a coffee shop, where many of us spent more time than was prudent. We either stayed inside, pretending we enjoyed the mud that was coffee, or we loitered around outside when the weather allowed, leaning on our cars, talking like the experts we were on all subjects. The cars we drove were older than we were, but we were grateful to have them.

Walking to school in the winter, especially as teenagers, was the epitome of uncool. And, of course, we were cool, even if there was nothing cool about us. We were alike in many ways—similar in background, experiences, and socio-economic status. We stuck together, sometimes to our detriment.

I remember him well, as the scar carves a deep memory. Like many of us, he would hang out at the coffee shop, or outside by his truck while waiting for a class to start. He was charming, not that he knew it. His smile was perpetual, and he always had kind words. His thick, straw-blonde hair waved as he went by, and his tender brown eyes were often at ease. Tall, lean, and muscular —a true cowboy. But even with his athletic physique, he was not interested in school sports. He was not aggressive in any way.

On the outside, he was the epitome of the well-balanced, grounded teenager, yet far humbler than his peers. And he was smart. He had insight and wisdom beyond his years, things he had learned from his life's rocky path. He knew his place in the world, but wasn't always comfortable in it. Yes, he struggled —as we all do. But unless you knew him intimately, you would never know of his demons, demons in the eyes of others, which he ultimately embraced as his own.

When he would come upon us, he would announce himself.

"It's just me," he would say, assured that he was no one to get excited about. Even he was convinced that he was not special in any way. But he was wrong. The inner magic that we all once had, until life's experiences wore it away, had gone in him at an early age. Little did he know, he was still magical. I saw it in him, like the suntan that radiated from him as he fussed with the engine of his jalopy. He was often shirtless when the weather allowed. His rodeo-riding physique sported a tattoo of a bucking bronco just above his waistband on one hip and a tattoo of a lasso on the other.

Rust and red, his grandpa's old pickup truck, was his pride and joy, despite the ridicule he suffered when he stepped down from it. His grandpa's cowboy hat, a worn leather spectacle, hung from the gun rack in the cab. It was something to behold—dirt and grime from many years on the trail. A pinched crown with a wavy brim and miles of wear added to its legitimacy. He had inherited both the truck and the hat from his grandpa, who had passed years ago.

He would often get harassed by adults in the building and sometimes by students who thought a little too highly of themselves, all because he stuck out in our urban setting. And they were not shameless about it in any way. He was a young cowboy, lost and trying to find his way in an unfamiliar environment. Our town couldn't have been more different from where he had come from: someplace in Tennessee, where they like pick-up trucks, cowboy boots and hats, confederate flags, and shooting pistols. Some adults saw him as a likely problem. He would say that none of that bothered him and confessed that he really didn't know why he was being given a hard time. It was a diverse student body, with kids having more in common than not.

He looked out of place in his cowboy hat and boots, with a prominent white Skoal ring in the rear pocket of his tight, faded jeans. Strange that his chewing tobacco never came out of his pocket. He wore a replica of a six-shooter as a belt buckle. He spoke with a slow drawl that matched his easy-going demeanor. He walked with exaggerated slowness. He drove his beat-up, old pickup truck with Tennessee plates. The administration would not give him a parking permit. The admin in charge of parking said that his truck wasn't road-worthy, so a parking permit was not going to be issued, unfair and untrue as it was.

Yes, he had a tough time fitting in. He was, in fact, different, but not in a way that others would have known. It emphasized his uniqueness as well as his separateness from others. He confessed that he felt different from those back home as well. He was who he was, and he was proud of his Southern heritage. But he believed that who he was contradicted who he was supposed to be. Misplaced as he was in this school, some were willing to accept him. Those who gave him a tough time didn't try to get to know him. But I did, and we became intimately close.

What made him different wasn't what others were able to see. It was what they couldn't see, what he was feeling deep inside, which he couldn't share openly. He knew he wasn't alone in how he felt, this world inside of him. But it wasn't what his lineage represented, and he knew it. He came from a long line of rough-and-tumble cowboys. Real men. His was a mental battle for survival and the emotional need to succumb, having a passion he could not control and did not understand.

I had sought him out. He greeted me with a friendly southern drawl. Initially, he seemed understandably confused about my intentions but became cool with them. We had a special untranslatable language of subtle gestures, winks and nods, odd allusions, and flirtatious words. His smile was soft and sweet as we passed in the halls. The unfamiliar wouldn't know what was behind that smile, what it truly meant, or to what it would lead. Only the familiar would know. Only those who shared similar passions and needs would know.

Only he and I would know.

Our liaisons would reinforce and motivate our desire for one another. Dopamine would be released when we anticipated the behaviors that led to intimacy. Our high would only last so long though, before we needed each other again. Each time he would give in to his demons, he would say it was breathtaking, life returning to his core.

His past was deeply personal. He and I had not shared a similar past. But we came to share each other. He held no resentment of our relationship, was grateful for our experiences together, and was thankful for not having to be alone with his feelings. When we shared each other, physically and emotionally, life seemed better for him, if only briefly.

But then the mental battle would return.

His mom, whom I knew from my visits to their apartment, was expecting the worst from the school community, as her experiences over the years had led her to anticipate. She wasn't disappointed. His dad, she never mentioned, so I never asked, but I knew.

For much of that year, as I remember, he would get hassled by some of the adults in the school. They treated him as the resident outsider, associating him with some of the unfavorable incidents in the building, none of which had to do with him. They couldn't pin him on any inappropriate behavior aside from being peculiar. He tried keeping a low profile, but he stuck out everywhere he went. He seemed different enough to be considered one for trouble, but doing wrong just wasn't him. Some of the adults would keep an eye on him. He couldn't walk down the hall without having one teacher or another track where he was going, watching him from their assigned posts.

We saw the whole thing with a little exaggeration and comedy. He led us to believe that he had experienced this same treatment in the past since moving north. He did speak fondly of his school years in Tennessee. A victim of bigotry and intolerance, he struggled with his own demons as well, as if that weren't enough.

His mom knew of her boy's internal conflict. She worried as mothers do, as mothers always have. Her words, meant to ease his pain, had little effect on the relentless torment driving him.

He occasionally spoke of his father, a rodeo celebrity skilled in using a lasso. He wondered if this was an inherited struggle, and if it was why his father engaged the rope that one last time when the same demons his son struggled with were too much for him to bear. A legacy his son would have to live with until he chose not to.

My friend died on a cold, cloudless night in January. The story goes that he took his grandfather's gun, inherited before leaving Tennessee, behind the garage apartment where he and his mother were living. She had heard the gunshot. She got up to check on him, and she noticed that the light was still on in his room, but he wasn't there. Fearing the worst, she went outside to look for him. She found him with a self-inflicted gunshot to the head, his grandpa's cowboy hat beside him.

What we knew for sure was that he took his own life. The details didn't matter. It was a tough time for those of us who knew him. It was an incredibly challenging time for me. We had become as close as two boys were able, given the fire that burned between us.

I visited his mom when I heard the news. Her eyes were sad and tired. She was packing their belongings into moving boxes. I didn't ask why. According to her, he grew up in a small southern town where the stigma around suicide is forceful. She had learned that his remains would not be allowed in any consecrated ground or hallowed plot but beyond the churchyard and cemetery walls where the suicide and un-christened go.

"Where I come from," she said, "someone *commits* suicide because it's considered a crime and a sin. And churches don't let people who did it be buried in their cemeteries."

She struggled to maintain her composure, though she failed. To say that she was grief-stricken was an understatement. She was now alone in this world, and she was returning to her small southern town without her 17-year-old son.

"He was a kind and loving person, now gone forever," she said.

I knew this to be true. He was kind and loving, and in ways no one really knew. He was beautiful and pure as a dream but just as fragile and easily torn. She knew of our affection for one another and expressed gratitude for it.

"He was trying to find himself in this new environment," she told me.

I knew that finding himself would have been difficult for him, given who he was and where he had come from. But he knew as I did that it would have been even more difficult in a place like Tennessee.

"Maybe he was bullied," she said. "If no one liked him, it was because they didn't know him."

All I could think about was the unbearable pain his mom was suffering, and I knew that it was the result of narrow-minded bigotry and the social and religious norms that dictated the times. He was young, beautiful, and blossoming.

Now and then, I would think of him and allow myself to feel the need for a touch or a word from him to fill the moment's ache. But I would have to put away that ache, and it would leave an echo—the blank, unfilled shock of a craving deferred.

Our tender moments have become elusive as a forgotten dream, replaced by the horrible, heavy crush of heartache and grief. And upon feeling the pain once again, I would yell out the most outrageous things. Some of it was pure hatred of the injustice. Some of it was the hostility and regret I bottle up inside and never give voice to, until the pain wrenches it out of me. Then I would fall silent, mourning what was gone and would never return, the way the years slipped away, robbing us of our pleasures, the love and the lust that seared us.

Section II

Anthony's Sin
a novella

by Jack Cooper

Although this story is biomythographical, the names and other identifying characteristics have been changed.

Contents

My Story

The pain of losing someone I loved is the price of all the joy he brought me. The more it hurts, the more it seems directly proportional to the depth of the bond we shared, our experiences, and our understanding of who we were together. The pain has dulled somewhat, but it will always be there, like the black boulder of grief inside my heart, ready to make itself known. It's odd to think about this now and realize it all took place in just two years. It doesn't seem possible that so much could happen in so short a time. It was a whole different world then.

Given the complexity of our surreptitious relationship, I was so devoted to him. I had such an intensity for him. The circumstance of his absence left my emotions in complete limbo. He was gone, and I became stuck with all this love for him. Where was it supposed to go? It wouldn't turn to hate or loss or indifference, and it wouldn't simply go away. Was I to follow him to that "ultimate end" he spoke of and eventually chose? If I did, what was shared between us would fade.

So I instead became the keeper of memories. Who else would ever know of us? Letting those memories go would surely guarantee that we hadn't happened, as if we, as one, had never occurred. My love wouldn't end. It became an ode to him; it continues to be an ode to him. Is that grief? Or is that the inability to process grief? Is telling our story finally a way to grieve, let go, and finally heal?

◊

My adolescence before meeting him was spent waking up sick every day with pure depression and absolutely hating life. I longed for this one earthly pleasure, and I craved to taste it more than any other desire.

I would close my eyes to it, hoping it would disappear. It did not. Not ever, not even temporarily. The cruelty of a god was conspicuously absent in moments like these. There would be the tormenting sense of anticipation, the sudden anger, the irritation toward other people, and the complicated feeling that the missing piece was just around the corner.

I could only keep going and do the next thing, even when I didn't have the strength or desire to go on. I felt distant from my family, and whether they felt distant from me, I didn't know. They would not have understood what went on inside me, and I stopped caring about whether or not they did. I knew every day that I could die, and this helped me. Eventually, I would have to succumb to the risk of satisfying that craving or choose to die.

◊

I had turned 16. It was before digital technology. No cell phones. No personal computers. No internet. We knew the time of day from a watch on our wrist or a clock in the car. Our rock-and-roll played on 8-track tapes much louder in our vehicles than was allowed at home. It was a time when a guy's hair was as styled and tended to as any girl's. Home phone landlines were for the adults in the house, available to us teenagers only for brief minutes when not in use. We memorized dozens of telephone numbers, dialing them all by hand.

Growing up outdoors and exploring our community was our Google Maps. Our social media was engaging peers in the halls of the school, or on one street corner or another in the neighborhood. Our chat room was when we were smoking in the school bathrooms.

Social networking was whenever the next party or gathering happened. We would consume excessive amounts of alcohol before we reached the legal age to do so and smoke dope before the law allowed. The Vietnam War was ending. It was the seventies, before the rainbow flag and the PRIDE movement.

Before Him

The war and the threat of being drafted were essentially over. Some neighborhood boys did not return, as indicated by the gold star in the windows of their family homes. I grieved for those who did not return, the ones I had some affection for before they left. At 16, I was concerned about seeing my life moving forward without wearing a uniform. Second from the oldest, I had other plans. Although I admit, I was intrigued by being among other healthy young men in close quarters. Mom still insisted that her brood enter the military upon graduating high school. I think that was her way of lessening her load, one by one.

We think we have control over our lives, especially when we are young and seemingly invulnerable. Little did I know, I had no control over anything.

"I'm going to college," I would say, not that I believed it.

Mom responded frequently, "You can attend college for free in the military. How else could you afford college? And if you go to West Point, the government will give you a car when you graduate."

As ridiculous as that sounded, I didn't waste my breath challenging it. The last thing I needed was to leave a militant mom for armed services mothering. I let her make her noise while I muttered something sarcastic, usually triggering one of her ugly psychotic outbursts.

"Yeah," I'd respond, "but getting killed for free is also a possibility. What would a free car do me, then? No, thank you. Besides, your friend Sarah was killed flying home with a plane full of Vietnamese kids. Operation Babylift crashed and burned with only a few survivors. I'll take my chances in a uniform of jeans and T-shirts."

"You kids don't know what the hell is good for you," was her canned response.

"Oh, but I do. You go in the military," I would say under my breath.

That was the start of many days with my single-parent mom of five kids. I was driving, working, and feeling somewhat liberated. Whatever reason I could come up with for not being home worked for me. I needed to figure myself out, and so far, I was not doing well figuring anything out. But then, he came along.

It was typical of boys like us. So wrapped up in who we were or should not be. We didn't think the world held a place for our kind. We were often on hypervigilance, hiding what really made our hearts pound. Those unnamable feelings.

When it came down to it, I didn't understand him or myself at the time. I thought I might finally figure it out if I wrote it down as best as I could remember. But I can't get enough of it down. There are always more fragments of memory coming back a little at a time. And what I've written does not begin to explain it. And so, the longer I go on, the harder it becomes to understand anything about those years.

❧

The chronological sorting of memories is an interesting challenge. My time then is distant and blurry, except for my time with him. Although we had so many happy days, they sometimes merge into a sweet and indistinct blur. But that may just be how I want to remember those days. My thoughts of him may be idealized due partly to the intense feelings and emotions we had for one another. It would all come together—my future, my past, the whole of my life. I might have had any number of ways to speak about him, but this is the only way I will ever do so.

Spring - Year One

Dad was good enough to let me have his leftover Chrysler. Of course, I had to guilt him into it. With a car and friends from the neighborhood, my mission became figuring out who and what I was. Smoking dope and drinking eased the anxiety of really knowing what I was. Staying under the radar was an absolute necessity. My peers never knew my affliction, so I thought anyway. I referred to it as an affliction then, as it was a time before the rainbow. Although I had a wide circle of acquaintances, intimacy of the kind that interested me was almost non-existent.

We were an odd mix. Just a neighborhood group that would gather almost daily. Usually within the same several city blocks, occupying one street corner or another. Mature trees everywhere, entirely residential. Cornhill. That was our neighborhood and the limits to our roaming. It would all change when one by one, we all began driving.

We were throwbacks from Teddy Roosevelt School K-8. We all lived within several blocks of the school and had attended it for most of our years. Although we had moved on to one of six high schools in the city, three public and three Catholic, we still gathered as a group to share the daily snippets that made up our teenage lives.

Julia was shy, so much so that I found her endearing. She was gentle and kind—a petite girl with long chestnut hair, brown eyes, and lovely lashes. I would walk her home, glad to be in the company of someone so pleasant and cheerful, before making my way to the erratic sanctuary that was my home. I looked forward to spending time anywhere and with anyone before having to head home alone, a journey I seldom looked forward to. Julia presented a peaceful and calm friendship. I needed it before arriving home, where peace and calm rarely existed.

Just after my sixteenth birthday, on one of those days, it felt like spring—blue skies, puffy white clouds, warm breeze. I walked Julia home as I often did. On this occasion, she invited me to meet some of her family.

"My mother and father aren't home, but my brother is, and maybe my grandmother," she revealed.

"Okay," I replied, although I did not see the point in these introductions. But since going home was my only alternative, I agreed.

Her home was a gray wood-frame two-story that was typical of the neighborhood. The street was lined with mature oaks, tall maples, and majestic chestnuts here and there. All the branches were still bare from the winter. Streetlights and utility poles, all tied together by power lines. The front porch, with its tall white columns, was the width of the house. On the second floor, sitting atop the porch, was a sunroom that looked out onto the street and walkway. We climbed the porch stairs to the unlocked door, and as she went in, I followed close behind.

The dimly lit foyer presented a heavy oak pocket door, which lead into a living room with a single table lamp dressed in a silk rose lampshade with swaying fringe. The rooms were saturated in rich oak trim. Ivory walls adorned with black-and-white framed pictures. It oozed warmth, comfort, and age. A worn wool carpet lay on the oak hardwood floor, and vintage furnishings filled the room. A large crucifix hung on one wall just above a table cluttered with various religious artifacts and palms from the Sunday before. Immediately in front of us was an oak staircase with a carpeted runner. The smell of cooking with garlic drifted in the air, mixed with a faint scent of church frankincense and myrrh. Julia shared that her grandmother lived in the downstairs rooms, but we did not see her. She was widowed for most of Julia's life and had always shared the same home as Julia and her family.

I followed Julia as she ascended the staircase. The wall from the first-floor foyer to the second-floor landing was lined with framed portraits. Julia saw that the pictures had my attention and took the time to identify several of them as we climbed the stairs. The first, prominently displayed, was Pope Paul VI. The few that followed were pictures of her maternal and paternal grandparents. There were three pictures, all in black and white, of angelically posed children dressed in white, one boy and two girls. Pictures of Julia and her siblings' first Holy Communions. I saw three individual ink-black silhouettes of Julia and her siblings completed in first grade.

We chuckled as I recalled my siblings and me having it done by our first-grade teacher. Three more pictures followed, showing the siblings adorned in their Catholic Confirmation robes. At the top of the stairs, the landing led into the sunroom at the front of the house. The music of the Electric Light Orchestra emanated from within.

When we entered the sunroom, there basking in sunlight stood Julia's older brother, Anthony. He was smiling wide, and his bright white teeth shimmered. His eyes had a devilish spark as if proud of some unknown accomplishment that only he knew of. I melted to my core, my heart bumping and thumping. Slender he was, so young and beautiful, if ever a boy can be that handsome.

With a shy smile, he said hello as Julia proceeded with the proper introductions. He and I stood there gazing at one another, captivated, neither willing to break the spell. Julia ended the trance by announcing that she was going across the way to visit with her friend Janet and would return when her parents arrived home from work. At that, she departed the room and descended the stairs. Awkwardly, we watched Julia through the sunroom's many windows as she marched across the road to Janet's home.

He and I stood there for a moment, and he flashed me a smile that I felt down to my groin. I had no idea how he meant for me to take that smile. I had no idea whether he meant anything more than friendship by it. I had no idea what to do with it. It was fascinating and not the least bit unwelcome.

At that moment, my life was altered. Suddenly, something I had kept at arm's length for as long as I could remember was standing before me, and I could not get past it. It was just there, needing to be dealt with.

"I was listening to ELO," he said. "It's one of my favorites, although I'm more into jazz. I'll turn it down so that we can talk. Glad you were able to come by. My sister has told me that you sometimes walk her home."

"Uh, yeah," I replied, speechless as I was.

I tried to understand what had just occurred but became distracted by his open flannel shirt, the sunlight gleaming on his smooth chest and small tummy, and his well-worn, snug-fitting jeans outlining his slim waist, round bottom, and slender legs. I was beyond delighted to be with him. I gazed into his eyes as he spoke, probably looking the fool, lusting after this older boy while he talked and I listened. I didn't care how it seemed.

I prayed he wouldn't need to leave, to go tend to some pressing, older boy concerns. I didn't want him sending me on my way. But he proved to be perfectly willing to occupy his time with me. I didn't know it yet, but this boy would become my intimate new friend—quiet, clean, and pure.

Anthony, a shy host at first, offered me a place on the carpeted sunroom floor, as there was no furniture in the room for me to sit on. The walls were painted lemon yellow, appropriate for a southwest-facing sunroom. It had a closet to one side, a clothes rod running the length of it that buoyed cold-weather outerwear. In one corner of the closet floor was a short stack of what appeared to be textbooks and notebook paper. In the other corner, hanging on a hook, was a JROTC uniform, neatly pressed, bearing a nameplate, honor star, and a Catholic school crest. The room had two outside walls lined with windows and no source of heat that I could see or feel. Brisk as it was, I sat on the carpet, my jacket tossed nearby. He sat across from me, and we faced each other as we stumbled along through small talk. He sat very close to me, so close that his breath, sweet as mint, tickled my cheek.

"I've been looking forward to meeting you for a long time," he said.

I looked away, surprised by his frankness, silently flattered and excited. Then I realized he was waiting for me to reach out and receive what he was offering. His eyes were laughing, watching. And then I felt it. The flicker grew steadier inside me. Exploded in me. I was sensing that he, too, shared those same unnamable feelings. I didn't have to wait to feel joy. Quietly, suddenly. Like a wave swelling in my chest.

Over time, our small talk gave way to more heartfelt words, and a level of coziness just short of intimacy began to develop between us. While we were getting to know one another and moving into more genuine conversation, he confessed that he had encouraged his sister to bring me to meet him. He revealed that he would often watch me walking his sister home from the windows, observing me as I turned to leave.

I had just learned the root of that devilish spark in his eyes that I had noticed when I first arrived. But then there was something else in his eyes—a gentleness, a knowing—which made me feel somewhat exposed and vulnerable. I would remember, on occasions, having the sense of someone being onto me when I wasn't ready to admit to myself that they would be right in their presumption.

But now I was flattered, hopeful, and excited. He leaned in and gave me a gentle, minty kiss. A kiss from a beautiful older boy! I thought I would lose any sense of coolness I pretended to have. I was a little embarrassed to have been enchanted by him. Our hours spent together that day became the first of many days we would idle away, lying on the sunroom floor, learning of each other's secrets, and realizing we weren't alone in this world of ours.

When our small neighborhood group gathered, Julia would let me know that Anthony would be home from campus and hoped

I would be by. For my own selfish reasons, I would never disappoint. Nothing would get in the way of my growing affection for Anthony. I often avoided home, so getting phone calls from there was hit or miss. The days he and I spent together led to our blossoming relationship. His parents were at work during the day. His grandmother was downstairs, frequently cooking and, in the beginning, letting us be. Julia was always at Janet's until her parents arrived home.

We explored each other in ways I never knew possible—mind, body, and soul—learning each other's darkest secrets, uncertainties, and hopes for the future. The rush of joy and fear, the shame and thrill of our forbidden bond, the secret that twined us together.

I loved watching him while he stood naked at the sunroom windows. I can still clearly picture how it felt, experiencing the little truths of the moment as though it were still happening in the present, preserved in my mind: he is 20 years old. He is unafraid here in the sunroom. He is not careful here in the sunroom. I saw no instances of unhappiness, tension, or darkness. Here, he allowed me to feel his heart, feel his breathing, and taste his innocence, and we were allowed to be as one.

This feeling began to grow in me. I can only describe it as a stirring—powerful yet hidden deep within. And I welcomed it, feared it, embraced it.

The mere thought of him and his beauty, of how he filled me with awe and set my head brimming with hope, made me flush like a boy in the thrall of new love. His skin was neither white nor brown but a sun-kissed golden glow. Smooth and warm and as perfect as a boy can be. His dark hair and sweet brown eyes were a family trait. His slender waist and strong legs, his developing chest and shoulders, his arms strong enough to hold me, and hold me they did. Lying next to him, feeling the rise and fall of his every breath, listening to his beating heart, breathing in the scent of his innocence, often wearing nothing more than his small gold cross on a fine gold chain. His face radiated. I wished it could last forever. He could be devilish and feisty and, at other times, tender and fragile. Pure, too; no meanness in him. No spite or evil. A boy angel. A dream come true—a first love. The pain and grief were yet to come, forever destroying the hope Anthony had introduced into my world, our world, a world where I had once believed I would always be alone.

❧

It was still spring, but it was cold. A few fine flakes of dry powdery snow seemed to drift onto the car's windshield as I drove. We had arranged to meet at his house when my classes ended for the day. I parked a short distance from his home, being cautious for reasons that weren't clear to me. I walked to his home in the softer light of the late afternoon. Although I was excited to see him again, my thoughts were foggy, gray like the bark on the trees. A consequence for getting sloe-gin drunk the night before. I needed sleep. But I needed him more.

He waved from the sunroom windows as I approached, and he greeted me downstairs at the front door. He was wearing nothing more than a pair of tight-fitting, worn-out jeans. He looked beautiful as he took the stairs to the sunroom two at a time. I followed just as quickly.

We kissed, one of those soft, beginning-of-relationship kisses. With patience, he will trust me, I thought, and he will show me his plumage. If I rush him, he will fly away. But slow didn't happen. His plumage was displayed as we slowly removed our clothes and embraced under a blanket. The blanket shrouded his face, but I could sense him watching me.

❧

We took turns smelling each other's skin. Sensory notes. Tastes. Textures. I held his face in my hand. Sunlight cut through the sunroom windows and illuminated his eyes and sparkling smile. He grabbed my waist and pulled me against him, and we briefly shared another kiss. My hands were in his hair, and his hand was behind my neck as he pulled me closer. We inhaled each other's exhales. Go slow, I thought, but neither of us moved slowly. We exploded on each other.

At some point, we fell asleep. When I woke, his arm was placed over me, his nose burrowed into my neck. When I moved, he pulled me closer. I got up to leave, wanting to stay. Go slow, I kept thinking.

"Sorry, but I should be going," I said.

He shrugged, then smiled. "We'll be together again," he whispered. "It's better to go slow." He read my mind. He placed his hand on my back, and I wrapped my arm around his neck, and we held each other in our own little world.

I felt the pulse of his heart as I gently placed my lips along the artery of his neck. His warm skin, kissed by the sun, was smooth against my face. I tried to leave again, hoping he would keep me from going. Again, he read my mind and wrapped me tight in his arms. He nuzzled his face against my neck, and I took in his scent like an addiction. And I realized then that this is how it is supposed to be. This is the real me. This is what I have longed for, craved for, for as long as I can remember, without knowing what it was.

We were standing at the top of the landing as I prepared to descend the stairs and leave. "I'll walk you down," he said. But his hands were still around my waist, my hands on his chest, and our foreheads were touching. Our eyes were making bold plans. Devouring each other. Moving in together. Meeting each other's families. Sharing a life.

He is sweet, I thought. Like peaches, his aftertaste was so pleasantly overwhelming, and it lingered. His touch ignited something in me that had always remained under the surface but was knowable, a growing heat ready to scorch my world. Our souls had spilled out through the slightest touch. This was how it breached the surface. I had been cold for so long that I didn't know what human warmth felt like. I had accepted my bleak, icy future. Then he and his warm breath touched me. I was almost too frostbitten to know I had been touched, but instinct told me something different. It burned. It burned so magnificently that my being had become inflamed. No one's essence could have unraveled me as easily as his had. He was my rebirth. He gave me the strength to rise.

So much for going slow.

Summer – Year One

The sun shone in through the open sunroom windows. A light breeze barely moved the shades, rolled up high. Anthony stood barefoot in his uniform, looking perfect as ever. It was a uniform left over from cadets who had passed through his Catholic school years earlier. The blue service uniform with red cording on the trousers hung on him as if it had been tailored perfectly to his frame. His nameplate was pinned just below the school crest. He looked different with it on… more mature, proper, and handsome.

As he released the brass buckle and removed the belt, he bemoaned his choice to attend a school that he felt was less of a choice and more of an expectation. A life of inhibition and missed chances, perhaps, but also a bearable life, a life that we both had chosen and, to some extent, continued to choose. As he removed his uniform, I then saw the boy whom I had fallen for, the boy who welcomed me, welcomed who I was, and who I was to him.

He was not effeminate in any way, but he was far more beautiful without the uniform. He wasn't timid when declaring how he had always hated that uniform and what it represented, proclaiming that it was a rebuke of who he was. The uniform, which hung prominently in the sunroom, was always a source of consternation for him.

"Actually, how was it that you weren't drafted?" I asked. "So many gold stars in the neighborhood. Not that I'm not happy that you weren't. I'm happy you weren't drafted."

"I'll soon be 20, and my college status awarded me a deferment for conscription. I've never supported the war, and I'm glad it's over. But I wouldn't have served anyway," he answered adamantly. "I would have found a way not to." He would have found a way not to serve. He would become philosophical, at times, sounding more mature than the boy who lay naked beside me, warm and tender.

"You and me," he would say, "we're a secret. It's what we must be. Not really who we are. We become what we show to others. It's a lie, a uniform, which isn't who we truly are. We do it for them. We do it for us just to be able to live in their world. It's not right. It's not fair."

But I loved having something as wonderful as this that I need not—and could not—share with anyone. I never gave a damn about anything I learned in school, although I did learn. But this was the real world—this was real.

When I was expected, Anthony would greet me at the door. He would see me coming as he gazed out the sunroom windows, a big smile always on his face. On several occasions, his grandmother would be standing in the dim light of the threshold of her living room and foyer. Always in a black or gray paisley cotton dress, with a sweater on her shoulders. She wore no adornments beyond a black rosary wrapped in her hands and a silver cross around her neck, tangled in the billowing white lace of her collar, as it rested in the crook of her bosom. Her gray hair was pulled back in a bun. Her eyes, also gray, were piercing.

She would glare at me as if I had done something terrible to offend her. She was matronly and gave the impression that she could be a force to be reckoned with. Something about her made me look at her, then look away, then back at her, troubled at something. Something felt, not seen. Something emanated from her eyes, which was never there when I looked again to try to catch it a second time.

I would feel unwelcome, but not so that I would go away. I wondered what caused the disturbance she radiated so subtly. She moved quietly and talked little, if at all, and only to Anthony. Her voice was a mournful, ghostly drawl. She seemed to cast an invisible cloak of protection over him when I would enter, as if I were bringing him sin. Anthony ignored her even when she spoke to him. He would rush me up the stairs. As I passed by her, she made the sign of the cross.

We would relax on the light-colored, soft wool carpet… warm in the summer and cool yet comfortable in the winter. Shoes were removed on the landing before entering. Our clothes were in a jumble nearby, unnecessary until it was time to leave. The sun shone through the many windows, adding warmth, yet not enough in the colder months. When the weather was cool, a soft blanket was at hand, a welcome addition to the heat of our bodies hidden beneath it.

He emitted warmth. His skin felt soft and smooth. Sun-kissed and sun-sweetened. The long, dark lashes of his brown eyes tickled my cheeks. His chest moved in and out as he breathed. I felt his heart against my palm as it beat fast and strong. The excitement was building. He pulled me against his body, rested his head on my shoulder as he held me. One of his ELO albums played softly from another room. He sang quietly along to the songs. If I were being used, used to satisfy the urges of an older boy, my aggressive hunger for him and all that he could offer only validated what was happening. I felt a calmness come over me, an incredible feeling of bliss.

I was a boy in love. I felt a soothing warmth and clarity that I had never felt before. It wasn't that I loved the high of sex, per se, although I did. Very much so. But I remember thinking, this must be what it's like to feel normal.

Fall – Year One

The deep shade of the neighborhood cemetery offered some relief from the summer heat with its full canopy of hundred-year-old trees, their branches shimmying in the breeze and the leaves whispering above us. We were between seasons—summer and autumn—which meant that the lawns were fading, and the trees were starting to turn. We would lie in the shade under the oak tree by the crypt, which became our go-to place when desperation to be out of the house compelled us to venture outside the sunroom. The falling leaves provided bedding for our evening escapes among the gravestones. We knew how to make do.

❦

Labor Day crept up on us. The hours of sunlight slowly shrank, and the air became cooler because of it, bringing some reprieve from the fading summer heat. I looked forward to the relief of cooler days and nights, the first snows, and the crystalizing air. But the changing season also meant that Anthony was heading back to campus soon, which was devastating. Nothing I felt mattered anymore when he was gone, except during his return visits, which weren't nearly enough to satisfy my hunger for him.

We frequented the neighborhood cemetery for our alone time on those rare evenings we spent outside the sunroom. The gravestones dated back to the late 18th century. When we would stroll the neighborhood, Anthony could escape the watchful eyes of his family—nights at the cemetery afforded us the seclusion to be ourselves. I've since found solitude and peace among the dead. I did not know then that the weathered and moss-covered headstones would soon include the one that would bring me back there for years to come.

Gravel pathways would lead us to the Burke and Allyn mausoleum, the backdrop of our intimate moments. Erected in 1897 of granite blocks, the engraving above the solid bronze door read, "SAVIOUR IN THY PRECIOUS KEEPING, LEAVE WE HERE OUR LOVED ONES SLEEPING."

The alcove fringed with Corinthian columns provided a place to retreat, protecting us from the elements and, on rare occasions, from prying eyes. We would lie against our mausoleum under a grand oak that provided shade and cover, preventing nearby streetlights from shining upon our secret. Directly in front of us was the massive Sheehan memorial marker —a ten-foot granite cross sitting upon a three-layer plinth —a reminder of Anthony's Catholic upbringing and the guilt of his sinning. Here, we could express our natural inclination to be who we were to one another. The macabre setting of a graveyard at night was the price we had to pay at a time when our intimacy was reprehensible in the eyes of the zealots of purity. It was the time before the rainbow.

He would have uncomplicated wants, expressed them in his quiet, calm way, and rewarded me with smiles, caresses, and intimacy when I fulfilled them. I marveled at my good fortune: to have this slim, affectionate, beautiful boy with his simple pleasures, and yet to be embroiled each time in his boyish mystery anew. To be so close to him, to listen to the soothing beat of his heart, was a moment of pure happiness.

As quiet as it was among the memorials, grief was not silent. But we didn't let it keep us from doing what we needed and being who and what we were. We were intimate in a field of death, but it seemed so right, so fitting.

With our needs and pleasures fulfilled, he would become quiet, the quiet I knew to leave alone. And I would. Then he would sleep beside me, his chest rising and falling. I would study his nakedness until he stirred, and then it was time to leave.

⚘

It was an early autumn evening, and we walked around the neighborhood with the unspoken understanding that we were heading to the cemetery. The sound of the groundskeepers' lawnmowers would be silenced by early evening. A light wind moved through the autumn leaves, leaves that had not yet thought about tumbling to the earth. It was unseasonably cold. The neighborhood became a different place. The colors were so vivid, the air so dry and breathable that you wanted to consume it. We were quiet; birds chattered in the branches.

Upon crossing the cemetery's threshold, our eyes pointed toward the many flowerbeds stiff from an early frost. Wreaths and bouquets prettied the scene, still visible in the dusk. The funerals were over, and the groundskeepers were gone. Death loomed large among row after row of headstones.

I thought about all the tears that had fallen on this very same ground, of all the pain and all the goodbyes, but here we were, alone, to consummate our own pleasures and joy in life. Dead people would not disturb us or ask what we were doing there. They wouldn't judge or suggest that we should probably be doing something else, somewhere else.

In the shadows of moonlight, we made our way to the Burke and Allyn mausoleum. We settled by the grand oak. The crunch of dried grass beneath our feet silenced, and we thought we heard the barely audible whispers of the dead. We were uneasy, and the atmosphere of death and sorrow, in addition to the dim light of the evening, made us even more uncomfortable. But the darkness was a necessity for us. Things moved in the periphery—shadows, outlines, hallucinations our imaginations created. They all added to the already scary concept of the graveyard. The looming shadows sharpened our instincts and hindered our desire to relax into each other. We smoked a joint, hoping to calm our jitters.

As dusk turned to complete darkness and the joint seemed to relax us, nothing seemed spooky any longer. Now and then, a car or truck would rumble down the pothole-ridden streets that encircled the cemetery: Arthur Street on one side, Mohawk on the other, and the railroad tracks bordering the rest, which also ran along the yard of Anthony's home. Beaming headlights momentarily on the tall and short grave markers, making shadows move, would cause our vigilance to rise again. Then the vehicle would pass, darkness would return, and the stars scattered liberally across the sky reappeared. We were then able to focus on each other. It was time for just us.

We would lie beside *our mausoleum*, and our lips would find each other between the whisperings of sweet nothings. A catalyst to what would follow. It was in the graveyard where I would lay my tongue upon him. His subsequent moaning was befitting of the eeriness of the nighttime atmosphere among the dead. We found pleasure and joy among the whispers of the past where the living would grieve, shedding their broken-hearted tears. There, we would remain for hours at a time. And still, there was not enough time, not when a person becomes part of you. I could not imagine my world without him, for my life really didn't begin until the day we met.

❧

It was a brilliant fall day in October. It was one of the last summery days we had that year. By late afternoon, the cool air had begun to move in to stay. The trees and bushes swayed with a slight breeze. The sun filtered through the many windows of the sunroom. Now and then, an orange leaf sailed down from a giant maple that shaded the porch.

The house was silent, as it often was. We talked for hours, and I must have fallen asleep during one of the long silences between us. When I woke, he wasn't there. I knew not to go into the main part of the house—an unspoken understanding. I would lay very still for a long time. The sun filtered through the sunroom so faintly that I worried about it getting late. Eventually, I slipped on my jeans, shirt, and jacket and made my way downstairs, my feet creaking on the steps. The foyer had a sweet, musty smell. Absent was the frequent aroma of garlic and incense. It was so dim that it confirmed that the house was motionless, empty.

I found him sitting in one of the wicker chairs on the porch's shady side. Baskets brimming with leggy geraniums hung from the porch ceiling. He had on a T-shirt and a pair of jeans, and like most of the time, he was barefoot. He smiled, but not the smile of his relentlessly cheery demeanor. He had a book in his lap but wasn't reading. I sat awhile, knowing it would soon be time to leave. The silence was comforting, as it often was when we were together. It represented nothing more than the feeling of security between us.

As I was leaving, he asked, "Will you return later this evening?"

Those beautiful brown eyes of his pleaded in a way that I could never say no.

I eagerly responded, "Yeah, sure! Absolutely!"

That afternoon, the sky was fierce, burning blue, and the trees, ferocious shades of red and yellow. The first chill of the early snow that would fall that night was already in the air, but the incredible blue expanse was vast and exhilarating. The last summery day of the year was finally ending. The kind of day I loved the most. Autumn leaves would soon be giving way to the seasonal winds. The cold, gray season, sadly, just ahead.

It was dark when I arrived, and I couldn't see anything at first. The moon emerged from behind a cloud, and I noticed the first lonely snowflakes drifting down. Then I saw him, right where I had left him earlier that afternoon. He was looking at the sky, watching the lights from an airliner blink through the tree branches. The stars were endless and wouldn't disappear until sunrise. The night had a chill, the kind of chill that shivers the body, that he appeared to be enjoying. His fists thrust deep into the pockets of his jeans. He was wearing a light jacket, sleeves rolled up, pleased I had returned.

He greeted me, saying, "I was hoping you would come."

It pained me to think that he would have doubted my return.

We spent our evening as we spent our afternoons… in an empty house, lying together, intimately wrapped into each other, a candle burning in the dark sunroom. We shared our deepest thoughts, feeling comforted in the sometimes silence. It was as if the silence found the words for us, when our thoughts and feelings became too big for us to verbalize.

He was his usual sweet and gentle self. Attentive and loving. He was somewhat restored from his somber afternoon smile. He appeared much calmer, happier, and more relaxed. He was very talkative when he wasn't suffering from contemplating the future, but he sometimes had gloomy spells. I remember well the long, terrible days and nights following those occasions. I thought of him anxiously and often, worried that things may not be well with us. But he was most wonderful that evening, and I was reassured. The warmth of his nakedness, my security. His tight embrace, the promise that we will remain as one. Before the evening ended, the moon would fill the room with its milky luminescence, banishing the shadows, a sign that alleviated all my worries.

We sometimes talked about his family. Never mine. Often his grandmother, as she was a presence not too far from where we would seal our pleasures and the love and lust that seared us. Our conversations were mostly about who we were, how we felt, the feelings we had developed, and how we had to navigate our daily lives under the circumstances of our awareness. Sharing our thoughts of what may come had a dispiriting effect on him. So, if we stumbled on that topic, we would quickly refocus on the here and now. We shared an emotional and physical intimacy that was more tender and gentler than anything either one of us believed possible.

He mused aloud, "What if our innocence is destroyed? Is what we've become a sin? Would it go unpunished? I don't know. I can't figure it out. It feels so right, so natural. Maybe it's just the Catholic in me."

I couldn't respond to that. So, I didn't. It was confusing to me, too. Were we innocence destroyed? Sinners to be punished? And what did that really mean? A deep melancholy that would not lift for many weeks had already settled around him. And I know I had said earlier that he was perfect, but he was human, and he had human flaws too. He could be silly, which I loved in him, but he could also be worrying, which I thought unnecessary. But he could also be remote, when he pondered the conflict between life's possibilities and life's expectations. When he became remote in this way, my own melancholy would mirror his, and then it became something like alarm.

It was hard for me to think of him without romanticizing him. In many ways, I loved him most of all, if not only him, and it was he whom I was most tempted to flatter. It was one of the reasons I loved him —for that flattering light in which I saw him and he saw me, for the person I was when I was with him, for what it was he allowed me to be, what he allowed us to be. I loved him as though he were perfect, if only for me.

He once confessed that sometimes, when he wasn't with me, he would think about what was to come, contemplating the future — our future. Next week, next month, next year, and beyond. Where would we be? How would we do it? That thinking was difficult for him. His mind was trying to figure it out. It would frustrate him. It was a tree where the fruit was out of his reach. It made him unhappy knowing that our lives were filled with constraints, admitting that he had little control over the reality of things. A near-perfect elixir for pessimism —believing he had little influence over the social and religious norms he had to contend with. We were doing our best, just to keep to ourselves and keep what we had safe.

He admitted that when he was home and I wasn't around, he largely spent his time lying in bed trying to blot out all sense of consciousness. But for me, it was always hard to have bad days around him. He lit up my world like the rays of the morning sun.

"I wake up every day with nothing to look forward to but us," he confessed. "I just want to stay in bed."

"With me!" I would say, trying to make light of his pessimism.

"My grandmother is always on me like I belong to her. My parents work all the time, and we live in her house, as she often reminds us. She lets my sister be. I don't get it. It's as if I exist to replace my grandfather as her companion. It's making me nuts, and I can't do anything about it. My parents say not to make waves. I thought going away to school would help. But then you, and now I don't want to be away any more than I need to. But she's always there when I'm home. Wanting me for this and that, and church things."

I struggled to find something to say, something to do to ease his sense of gloom. Was I free to say what I was thinking? But he was not one to rock the boat. Not one to push back. I became his escape, but his sweet and carefree disposition was changing.

He went on, "If only we could move away together. Be who we are. I'm just so weighted down. I don't know what to do. I considered transferring back here to finish school, but it would be closer to family, church, and obligations. I'd also have my comings and goings more scrutinized and questioned. I can't win."

I had nothing to say about this, so I waited, but he said nothing more.

His pessimism had begun to worry me. It was not just his future that felt bleak to him. It was also our future that felt bleak to him. There seemed little either of us could do about the circumstances imposed upon us. He would darkly muse that he would likely never see the future that he wanted nor the future that was expected of him. He seemed stuck in a cycle of frustrating hopelessness. It was a twisted notion to think that his life revolved around the expectations of others, with him having little choice in the matter. He was feeling a deep anger and resentment well up in him as he contemplated what the future may or may not hold for us. Only then, in that very moment, did I see the pain he carried.

Outside in the street, the light was beautiful. It was the light of late autumn afternoons. It was an autumn day with a crisp wind that already hinted at the coming frigid winter. I looked to see him as he stood at the sunroom window. He waved me in, so I entered without him greeting me at the door. The wooden floors creaked as I stepped inside. As I climbed the stairs, I sensed his grandmother was not home. Absent was the heady scent of incense wafting out from her living area. I felt intrusive on those visits when his grandmother was in the foyer when I arrived. I was always glad when she was nowhere to be seen.

When I got to the top of the stairs and entered the sunroom, he was still standing at the window gazing out, barefoot, yet wearing his uniform. It was sunny beyond the sunroom windows. Sunny and calm. The leaves had gone red and gold for autumn, and a mild wind rustled them. Here and there, three or four leaves would swirl in the breeze before falling out of view. He was watching a bright red cardinal as it bounced between branches. There was a warmth, a softness over everything. Something seemed different about him, though I could not say precisely what it was—something in his manner, the quality of his silence, the focus of his gaze. Everything led me to believe that he was with me, but at the same time, he seemed to be elsewhere.

I asked, "Why are you wearing that uniform that you despise? Please, take it off."

He turned to face me and took it off, saying, "I just want a life that is more than what is expected of me." He would mention this almost every time we talked, though he would say it flatly, like a disappointing fact. "Let's not talk about it. I just want to hold you. I want to feel you. I want to feel us."

"Okay," I said, and he took me in his arms. The silence that followed was a bond between us, an intimacy. He and I would become one. And together, it was very natural. I could feel his feelings, suffer his sufferings. But also enjoy his joy.

We understood deeply the jumble of fear, lust, and joy that arrives with first love. Anyone who has ever been a teenager in love will recognize each swerve and lurch of the heart, often with a familiar wince. I was a teenager in love. We shared a yearning and desire that was so powerful and convincing—two beings who needed to be close together and become so immersed that each became the other. There was hunger, yet there was also the fear of satisfying that hunger. His insatiable eyes, his love on my tongue, and the sweet taste of his innocence seemed to be all I needed to satisfy my need for him.

We undressed, as we often did when we were together. We were lying down, and he climbed on top of me. I felt his lips on my neck, then his tongue over my nipples, and then his teeth, softly nibbling. I felt his hot groin sliding over my knee and down my shin. He drew my legs apart. He had me in his mouth. He didn't move. He just held me there deep. Then, bit by bit, his mouth rose up and down repeatedly. And then quickly, he was up and pressing his lips to my mouth. I slid into him fast and easily. He kissed my face and licked my lips. With his palms firm on my chest, we came, he on my chest and I inside him. As our heavy breathing began to slow, I softened inside him. Then, he slept beside me, as he often did afterward.

What we did and how we felt would bend us in all kinds of ways, until we were unfit for the straight life that was expected of us. We could have been many things had it not been for the curse of Catholicism and society. We were being denied the simple pleasure of being ordinary. To forbid the kind of love we felt destroyed our humanity. We had no idea where this would ultimately lead us, but I would happily travel with him through the gates of Hell for a future together.

When he woke, I knew it was time to leave.

"I can't stand being away from you," I would say to him. "Even being together isn't close enough for me. You're like a craving that I can't get enough of. And it's not just the sex. It's all of you. It just feels right."

His response was a bit concerning. "If this feels so right, why is what we do, how we feel, a sin? Aren't we meant for this? Why do they condemn us?"

I kissed his lips to quiet him, to distract him. To bring him to the here and now, away from the conflict in his mind. I would soothe him with caresses, kisses, and whispers. Yes, I was selfish with my needs, too, but I also loved him deeply.

He continued, "'Heaven is the ultimate end and fulfillment of the deepest human longings, the state of supreme, definitive happiness,' according to the Catechism. I wish we could close our eyes and skip to that 'ultimate end.'"

"That's Catholic jargon, Anthony. I don't buy it. Not any of it. I'm sorry."

"It's easy for you. I get it. I'm struggling with it. It's the faith I was raised on. Why can't they accept us?"

"I was baptized and raised Catholic," I responded. "I learned how to pray the Our Father and Hail Mary to say the rosary. I made my first Holy Communion and was confirmed at the Blessed Sacrament Church. I attended Sunday mass and religious instruction once a week for years. I went to confession, so that a man in a robe hiding in a dark box could ask me questions about my dirty thoughts. And for all that, I learned what complete bullshit the whole thing was."

His grandmother's presence was just one floor below, her ear at the bottom of the stairs, stairs that led to our intimacy. She was an ever-present reminder that what we were, what we were doing, and how we felt were all being judged by the Almighty Himself: Anthony's grandmother, the chosen conduit from us to Him. Anthony would murmur his sweet nothings—whispers between us alone, so that Grandmother and He wouldn't be the wiser.

❧

It was a beautiful day. Bright and warm, with no breeze but no overbearing sunshine either. It was a perfect day to go for a walk. As we walked along, I was sneaking glances at his handsome face, and he caught me admiring him. He smiled. Then he did the most unexpected but natural thing in the world. He turned to me, took me in his arms, and pulled me to him.

"Kiss me," he said. His face radiated pure delight, wild with serene beauty. I shook my head no, dismissed the idea, and looked around. I knew we were not alone. Standing no more than some yards away was an elderly couple from the neighborhood, walking hand-in-hand. Anthony had let his guard down. Threw caution to the wind. It was so unlike him. Encouraged as I was, I didn't understand his rare impulsiveness.

Winter – Year One/Two

The day was sunny and clear. The air had warmed, and the early snowfall had melted. The sky was a perfect blue, with only a few puffs of white clouds. As I approached the front door to the foyer, I heard a voice that I knew was that of his grandmother. She appeared to have been lecturing him. As I reached for the door-knob, I paused to listen.

"It is wrong. So very wrong. You must atone. You must tame the shame of the flesh. We are not put on earth to please ourselves or pleasure each other but to be pleasing to God alone. Those who have allowed their demons to inhabit their lives—to sleep with them and wake with them and let them whisper in their ear— promise me…"

That was the last thing I heard before Anthony opened the door and motioned me in. Anger and anxiety mounted in my chest like an approaching storm. She looked at me with hollow staring eyes, wire-rimmed with spectacles. She never once spoke to me directly; her eyes said everything she needed to say. As was often the case in my presence when she tried talking to him, Anthony did not re-spond to her at all but rushed me up the stairs to the sunroom. She made the sign of the cross as I passed by her. I supposed later that, on some level, she had been expecting my arrival.

"Not sure how much you heard, but sorry about all that," he said.

"It's cool," I responded. But it really wasn't.

"We live in my grandmother's house, as she often reminds us. My parents are always working long, hard hours. It's as if she owns me. My parents are always saying, don't make waves. So, I don't. But lately, it's been hard. Today, she quoted from Romans, saying, 'For the wages of sin is death, but the gift of God is eternal life in Christ Jesus our Lord' as if I needed to hear that. What's wrong with who I am, really? I'm a good person. I'm having my doubts about so much lately."

As an unbeliever in a believing world, I needed to step lightly. Anthony was immersed in the believing world of Catholics— Catholic parents and grandparents, Catholic family, Catholic school, and maybe Catholic friends. He needed to keep the semi-abandonment of the rules of his faith sealed up and hidden from those near him, as if his breaking of some commandment was the end of life as he knew it. Anthony may have had doubts, but I sensed he wanted to believe. But he was conflicted with the faith that condemned who he was, who we were together.

His concern for us was not a simple one; it involved a dilemma between the fundamental truths within him. His feelings for me were complex. They could not all be boiled down to the love he was feeling but to what we were to become. At the time, I had no way of knowing it, and it would be years before I understood the nature and importance of his family and identity.

"Let it go, please," was all I could offer. I had not believed in his God for years. Nor any other god. I was contemptuous of such beliefs, but I was at the same time envious of his ability to remain tethered to his upbringing. I didn't want to be responsible for him having doubts, and I didn't blame him for his doubts either.

⁂

The drifts and ripples of winter snow had returned, revealed the landscape's artwork of the season's wind. The luxuriant trees of summer were long gone, having become bare and spindly under the winter sky. Spring and summer blossoms were awaiting rebirth within the cold, snow-covered earth. We were warmly dressed for our evening winter walk, an unusual break from our afternoon routine. Bundled in outerwear from head to toe, we walked with no place in particular as our destination. The wind blew cold from the north as we exhaled clouds of vapor. We talked about nothing of importance. But something was on his mind.

And then he asked me.

"I thought I would attend the Who concert in Buffalo on December tenth. If I can pull it off, would you go? Though I doubt you can."

"That would be a tough one for me. What day is it?" I asked, already knowing I would be unable to go.

"It's on a Wednesday—a school night for both of us. I'd be leaving directly from campus with some others who may go. I didn't think you could come. I'm not sure it's possible for me either. Just my luck, someone from home would call me that night at school, and I won't be there," he lamented. "Not sure it's worth the risk. And God help me if something goes wrong and we don't return to campus that night. I don't know. Maybe I won't be going. Not a big fan anyway."

He continued, "Although getting away unchained would be pretty exciting."

At that, the conversation ended. Given my circumstances, Anthony and I knew it would be impossible for me to pull that off. I had already been having difficulty at home with some of my disappearing escapades. He and I didn't share much on the social calendar, living the segregated lives we did.

The entrance to the neighborhood cemetery was upon us, and we invited ourselves in. We strolled among the snow-covered granite memorials. The sense of seclusion seized us, even as we were among the crowds of those who once lived. The silence of the dead was no longer a source of fear. If anything, the dead were a comfort. We pressed our cold lips together until they finally felt warm again. We were stealthy in our relationship, as it was forbidden. But our secrecy was exhilarating as it was risky. Humankind was not warm to our ways yet, even in the heat of the summer.

Spring – Year Two

Winter was shedding its gray hold, and spring was beginning its march toward summer. The days were becoming fresh, clear, and hopeful. But today, the clouds were heavy with rain that had not yet let loose. He was waiting for me in the cool April air. It was the beginning of our second year, and I told him so as he greeted me on the porch steps. He wore a cable knit cardigan, completely opened, exposing his smooth, bare chest and small, tight tummy.

As usual, he was barefoot at the bottom of his jeans. He smiled his beautiful smile, then suddenly stopped, and I saw his mind reeling back in time. He and I had lived through many afternoons in so short a time. Our lovemaking, our daydreaming, our hopes for the future. So often dismissed as an abomination by almost everyone in our combined orbits. He said he had good and not-so-good news for me, and I immediately sank into despair as I heard only that there was not-so-good news. My eyes brushed the floor, and he must have noticed my worry.

"You're bummed, aren't you? I can tell," he said.

"No, really, Ant. It's fine. What's going on?"

As we entered, the foyer smelled of furniture polish, incense, and the faintest whiff of lungo, strong black Italian coffee. We ascended the stairs to the sunroom two at a time, glad to be away from his grandmother's living quarters.

He wrapped himself around me as we entered the sunroom, ever so affectionate and loving. His ability to ease my fears and worries was always welcomed, and this day, he didn't disappoint. My trepidation of sad news was soothed by his gentleness, kisses, and caresses. He explained that he only had a little while for me today. Then, the clouds finally burst, and the rain began hammering the windows.

"I've got to go to a special mass this afternoon," he said. "It's a special mass called 'a day of Consolation.' I've got to take my grandmother. No one else is available, and she's insisting that I take her. I'm not able to get out of it. I'm going in uniform."

"Ugh. Okay. But you hate that uniform."

It was in the spring of 1976. Pope Paul VI, whom his grandmother worshipped, had been accused of a long-time gay relationship with Italian movie actor Paolo Carlini. The Pope denied it, and the Vatican's response was to have special masses of prayers on behalf of the Pope called "a day of Consolation."

If it seems odd that I offered no protest, I can only say that his way of reassuring me that we were still good and safe was all I needed from him then. And he assured me in the way he always did—with love, tenderness, and warmth. There was nothing I could do but give myself up to his embrace, nothing to do but abandon myself to his intimacy. It was enough to accept his presence as a gift.

Our love was marked with intense feelings of longing and attraction. We needed to maintain constant physical closeness when we were safe to do so. It was a need we shared: to embrace, flesh-to-flesh, exchanging each other's breaths, my face buried in the nape of his neck as I rested upon him. That was all it took to make him feel that the world would eventually yield to our way, and undeniably it satisfied my needs, too. Needs only he could fulfill.

As our time that day would come to a premature end, Anthony shared that his parents, grandmother, and sister were visiting Spencerport for a few days to visit with family. That was the other news. The better news was that he wanted to spend those days alone with me. The events of our first year, and the enthusiasm for his plan to spend a few days together, suddenly made it plain what was happening with us: we, as two-become-one, were becoming real. Hopeful.

When I came for him the next day, something seemed wrong. I could see it in him when I arrived.

"You seem agitated. What is it?" I asked.

"It's the fucking hypocrisy! It was at mass yesterday. The fucking priest and his sermon. He said some bullshit about the dignity of the human person and the sacredness of human life in all its forms. What about us in our form? What about you and I and who we are? Then he said, and I can quote him because it comes right out of the Catechism of the Church, which I was taught: 'question the beauty of the earth, the beauty of the sea, the beauty of the air…' And everyone responded, 'We are beautiful.' Like we're not beautiful, for Christ's sake? Like what we have is not beautiful?

"We're not supposed to question the teachings of the Church, but we should question the obvious truths of the earth, the sea, and the air. What the fuck? What illogical bullshit! And we are the ones considered an abomination? What happened to the dignity and sacredness of human life in all its forms? Such bullshit!" he said with disgust.

"I've never seen you upset like this, not ever," I responded. "I've never seen you angry. I've never heard you use profanity. It's more Catholic jargon, Anthony. Can you just let it go, please? I'm here now, please? I don't like you like this. I've never seen you like this. You're always wide-eyed and smiling when I come. You are always excited to see me. I don't like you like this. Please? What happened to you? What's going on here?"

I was getting very irritable, noticeably irritable. "You've never not been glad to see me. Let's just go, please."

"I'm sorry," he said. "I know. I'm sorry. I just want us to be okay. That's all. It's not right for them not to accept how I feel, what I feel, us. You know? I'm not a sinner! I love you. I love who we are together. Why is that so bad? Really? Why? I just want to be understood." His tone was still angry.

"It's not bad, Anthony. They've got it all wrong. They don't matter," I pleaded.

"But they do matter. That's the point!"

I knew what he was saying. Fear coiled around me, squeezing the air out of my lungs and making it hard to breathe.

"Please, just let it go. Please?" My eyes swelled with tears, and I tried to hold them back.

"I know, I know. I'm sorry. You've fallen hard. I know. I'm sorry."

He saw the hurt in my eyes, wrapped his arms around me, and whispered repeatedly, "I'm sorry." He buried his face into the nape of my neck, and I felt the tears rolling down his cheeks. The residue of his mood still lingered, and he went on about some of the lowest moments of his life.

Years of religious indoctrination lived in him, nourished him with its poison. With his religious beliefs and his emotions, I had to tread very carefully. Pain, like love, produces an overflow of feelings. He needed to be understood. We both did. But when we were not alone, our emotions needed to be bottled up, put under pressure, and tested against traditions, societal norms, and religious morality.

We took my car: a '68 Chrysler New Yorker, a family leftover. It was like driving a snow-tired living room, with a green leather interior and power everything. We discussed leaving my car behind and instead taking his, but that would be too conspicuous for his grandmother's neighbors. The summer cottage, frequently uninhabited this early in the spring, was located in the Adirondack foothills, less than an hour north of our small urban hometown. Anthony did schoolwork while I drove, and we listened to one of his Chuck Mangione tapes. We took the four-lane highway north, then veered northeast onto the two-lane that would bring us the remainder of the way. We were glad that the sun obeyed the weather forecast, shining brightly in a clear blue sky as we made our way to seclusion within the Adirondack foothills. Forests of pine trees along both sides of the road became more prevalent as we drove. Eastern White and other pines in thick clusters among craggy granite. The snow-banks along the side of the road were noticeably higher; winter had not yet begun to recede in these hills. As we approached the lake and turned off the paved main road past the Old Lake Inn, the dirt road to the cottage was still packed with snow. The inn's parking area had a few trucks with snowmobiles hitched to them. A giant town snowplow bellowing diesel exhaust was also in the parking area, but it was unoccupied.

When we came upon the cottage, it appeared to crouch low into a snowy embankment, as though it were trying to hide. Still, the chaotic pattern of its large slate roof was too flashy to go unnoticed. The cottage itself was made of stone, built halfway into a rocky slope, with a slit log deck. High in the blue mountain sky, the sun had warmed the slate roof and melted much of the snow there, causing it to slide off and block the entrance to the cottage door. Through the shade of the forest, we could see the rough, unevenly sized, grey stones that made up the walls. As we got closer, the occasional flash of color—some blues, others green or brown—became visible amongst the grey, and they looked like eyes trying to steal a glimpse of the world.

Despite the snow, spring was in the air. It felt cool, with just enough sun to energize your steps and wash the heaviness of winter away. Any passerby could see that Anthony was happy again, glad to be away from home. His stride was upbeat, and his smile beamed.

"This place looks cool," he said excitedly with a big smile. "How long have you been coming here?"

"Since I was a kid. But recently, it's been my getaway place since I started driving. But there is no running water this time of year. Pipes will freeze."

His puzzled look prompted me to clarify: "We're roughing it, Ant. We have heat, electricity, and a gas stove, but we heat snow on the stove for water, until the spring thaw when the well provides us water."

Anthony's laughter was reassuring. "I preferred we had running water. We can generate our own heat!" At that, we both laughed as we trudged our way to the cottage door, stumbling in the snow and still laughing excitedly, looking forward to our weekend adventure. The door swung open easily, and we flipped the switch that turned on the lights in the hallway, leading to the main room.

"I just need a few minutes to get the furnace lit and running. It'll be warm in about twenty minutes or so. Look around. Get comfortable. And I do mean comfortable!"

"Where do we put our stuff?" he asked as he explored the cottage.

"Wherever you want. No rules here. We're on our own. I like coming here when the family isn't. I'm to clear the snow off the roof and keep the path from the road to the door shoveled. This area is mostly uninhabited this time of year, so it's considered safe, and my mother doesn't expect any trouble. The snow removal work is hard, but having the excuse to escape from home on the weekends during the winter is worth it. My family's been coming here for years, so it is considered familiar and safe. For whatever reason, I'm considered the responsible one, number two in the pecking order of five."

I heard Anthony chuckle at that from the other room.

"Yeah, I know, right?" I responded to his amusement. "I'm glad they don't know the half of it! But it affords me these liberties I would otherwise have to fight for."

"Not me," he responded. "I'm kept close to home mostly, except for the school campus. They like to keep tabs on me." He laughed. "Especially my grandmother when I'm home from school. She thinks she's my religious, social, and moral keeper. I've always been her favorite, but as you know, it comes with a price. If I don't make waves or draw any questionable attention, they leave me alone for the most part. Well, until you, anyway!" At that, we laughed heartily.

Anthony was as honest a boy as I had ever met. He would never share us with his parents unless they asked him to; he said they had not. Anthony conveyed having no real need for their attention or approval; he could take care of himself, he told me. His independent mindedness surprised me, given his religious indoctrination and deep-seated fear of Hell.

I knew he treaded lightly at home. Life requires effort and will, and knowing when to make choices is essential. But it's also important to understand when not to make choices—to let things be. His honesty, or his inability to deceive, was honorable. Yet I sensed that it was only a matter of time before he would be pressed to reveal the nature of our relationship to his curious parents.

It had grown cold as the weak spring sun disappeared, but I had the furnace up and running, and the heat caused the wood-paneled walls to creak and pop as the warmth expanded throughout. Anthony brought in two big pots of snow that we put on the stove to melt for water. Although we had a functioning toilet, water was needed to flush it, and the melted snow was our only source.

It felt good to see Anthony in a relaxed mood, making light of his circumstances. With his rich laugh and quick eyes, he radiated the easy, good humor of a carefree and unburdened young boy. Although an adult by age, he was physically small, compact, quiet, and inward-oriented.

But this weekend, he was as excited as a Boy Scout on a camping trip. Our boots, socks, and jeans hung drying by the stove. He beckoned me to get close, to touch, to connect. We cozied up and enjoyed the additional warmth we could create for each other.

Wrapped in a quilt, we exchanged small whispers about nothing. When our bodies lay quiet, entwined in the darkness, we both quickly fell asleep. There was love-making, and there was love. This was love.

By late evening, we had woken up and become hungry, and I had to think of all the taverns in the few-mile radius that would serve warm food and cold beer. As I was built bigger than Anthony and looked older, I seldom had a problem buying alcohol. The drinking age was eighteen at the time, and Anthony had his college ID to prove he was of age. We were amused when proof of his age was requested, but not mine. So, at a tavern, we got cheap-beer drunk and headed back to the cottage. Once we were there, we had a silly, fun evening in bed, doing our best to keep warm under a summer quilt, the only cover available.

The next day, we hiked and explored the area, as we had nothing but quiet time to spend together; the land was still snow-covered, but spring warmth was beginning to emerge. He loved the natural beauty of the woodlands, admiring the bare deciduous trees and the green pines. It was exhilarating to spend time together outside the sunroom, even though we did spend it in the cottage just as we would have in the sunroom: just enjoying one another's presence. I spent much of my childhood here in this cottage and in the surrounding area, and I was well-versed in describing to him what it was like during the warmer months.

"There are ponds and woodlands and ferns everywhere. There are bullfrogs and spring peepers. That's a frog that supposedly chirps at the arrival of spring. There are plants like sphagnum moss, orchids, and pitcher plants everywhere. Birds that you don't see in the city, like herons and loons. There are raccoons and beavers. Otters and bobcats. Moose, black bears, and coyotes. There are several hiking trails, an old trapper's cabin, and a lean-to deep into the woods. There's an old cemetery with burials going back almost two hundred years. It's amazing here, from late spring to early fall. But the blackflies are vicious, usually until around the first week of July. Then the dry weather pretty much eliminates them. The first week of July is a turning point. Blackflies are gone, and the summer residents arrive. The evenings at the beach and the swimming are awesome!"

I may have spoken about the area too enthusiastically, excitedly thinking that we would spend more time here. I wanted Anthony to look forward to it with me.

As we walked through the fading winter wonderland, he asked, "Tell me about your family?"

Was I free to say no? I did not want to shut down our conversation, but I had to be honest in my response about family and the topic of faith, which would rear its ugly head from time to time. None of which surprised him.

"I come from parents of an early divorce after five kids, one right after the other. My mother had to make it under challenging circumstances. That left us on autopilot for the most part, which I appreciate, given that my whereabouts and what I do go mostly unaccounted for. Just the way I need it to be, especially since I started driving. Not that they would get the truth from me anyway, even if pressed.

"But I don't want to talk about my family. Their opinions and their interest in my life mean nothing to me. Their expectations are of little importance. Their disapproval and encouragement do not affect what I do or intend to do. I share nothing of value or importance with them."

As far as faith was concerned, he and I had on occasion discussed the subject. He wasn't shocked or scandalized or in some other way hurt by my revealing that I simply was not a believer in a faith that would condemn who and what we were. So, I told him again, "I was baptized and confirmed Catholic, as was my entire family, but I don't believe a word of it. Not the church's virtues, the Pope's purity, or the holiness of all those players in the so-called 'good book.' Not the existence of some all-powerful and loving god." He didn't reply right away, so I continued, "It's just not for me. You look at me surprised? You know how I feel about it. I don't accept the purity of the clergy—priests or nuns. The only thing pure about them were their victims."

"How do you know about that?" he asked, like I had just revealed a secret.

"We live in a small neighborhood, Anthony, with many churches, many kids. And kids talk."

The only thing that bothered him about us was that I wasn't bothered by us at all. For me, it was as natural as breathing. For him, it was happiness or damnation, and his happiness meant damnation. In my bliss, I didn't really grasp the amount of misery his family and faith were causing him.

"What about our future, not just our current escapades, given what is expected of us?" he asked.

I smiled at him, rejecting hopelessness. "I don't see us as an escapade, Ant." He smiled in return.

He admitted that he hadn't been able to think of a future beyond us. And perhaps his hunger for having a future with us nourished this idea. But did that mean there would be no future for him if there were no us? He was rarely diminished in spirit. But his thinking of what may or may not come to be disheartened me.

I wondered whether he could break free from his grandmother's oppressive religious adherence. This lifetime of being protected from evil by some divine principle. His family's generational legacy of fixed gender roles that only men and women complement each other. The Church's absolute prescription that conjugal relationships are only between the opposite sex. Would it be possible for him to rebel against a lifetime of indoctrination, against the teaching that the consequences for being who and what he was would be eternal and terrifying? His suffering from the constraints of a purity culture and maybe having a deep-seated fear of Hell was the damage caused by a lifetime of Catholicism.

As we made our way back to the cottage, we came across the carcass of a young deer. It appeared to have starved to death, as there were no signs of it being attacked by another animal. I explained that this sometimes occurred here, as winters were harsh and food for deer became scarce. I saw that it caused a heaviness in his heart, a lonely ache, a silent wound that I also felt and understood.

"At least it isn't suffering any longer," he stated with sadness.

My only thought was that Catholics treat death as an escape from misery. I didn't know at the time how true that would ring one day.

We sat around a campfire on our last evening in the north country. He tended the fire, adding new wood when needed, poking it with a large stick he'd found sticking out of the snow. Sparks flew up into the sky and disappeared. It was a cold Adirondack night. A sky without light pollution, it was both clear and dark, and stars radiated overhead. We were warming ourselves by sitting close, huddled beneath a surplus Army blanket, the wool keeping our body heat contained. With his head on my shoulder, we softly talked—thoughts of the last few days, intimate whispers, the quiet of the night, the hypnotic effect of the dancing flames. He whispered, "I'll soon be expected to take the obvious next step in my life."

"I don't know what that means, Anthony."

He sighed as he stared into the constantly changing flames. "Neither do I," he said. Then he and I and the night were silent.

The following day, the sun had come up and exploded with sunshine after a heavy snowfall during the night. The trees were glistening and covered in sparkles. The late-season snowfall created for us a winter wonderland. We packed up and headed home.

Anthony's source of sometimes private uneasiness was the matter of who and what we were. Not as two separate individuals, but that which made us one. Was it our age difference, he being four years older than me? Or was it our opposing views of faith and family? He may have been a struggling believer and a family devotee, even in different circumstances. Even so, the guilt that the Catholic religion fosters in its followers is often the last thing left as belief is challenged or ebbs away.

The age difference was often on my mind, as he could easily have moved on to someone closer in age and orbit.

I saw religion as a source of trauma, as he struggled to overcome the Catholic ideology's toll on his mind. We engaged in behavior that he had been taught was sinful to such a degree that the consequence of his so-called sin was Hell. I sometimes saw in him lightning bolts of guilt. I tried to understand his struggle.

Summer – Year Two

The late afternoon summer sun swelled through the sunroom's many windows. It hadn't rained in quite a while. The temperatures hovered in the eighties, and the humidity was brutal. The windows were open, but there was no breeze. The sticky warmth made our skin cling together wherever we touched. The July 4th weekend with the bicentennial celebrations was just days away. I suggested another weekend trip to the Adirondacks, where we could enjoy the Old Forge fireworks display and get some swimming in. I also hoped it would be cooler in the North Country. With sadness, Anthony explained why we couldn't escape for the weekend. "My parents are giving me heat. They want me to hit up the mayor for a summer job. I was always my grandmother's favorite, but I no longer know. I think she may be behind it. I wanted to take summer classes so that I could finish early. Last night's dinner conversation was about some guy named David Gray[3], who was beaten to death last October by the city police for being queer. His family was suing the city. My grandmother was glaring at me the whole time. Then she suggested I take her to the Saturday and Sunday masses for the holy days of St. Thomas and St. Elizabeth."

"I heard about Gray," I said. "We have a family friend, a cop, who said it didn't go down that way. Of course, he would defend his own. He said something about Gray being 'light in the loafers.' He got himself a good laugh out of it. I know what that means."

The July 4th weekend came and went, and Anthony was off limits doing family stuff. Frustrated as I was, I had become accustomed to taking a backseat to his family and religious commitments.

But Monday evening, July 5th, we had agreed to rendezvous by the abandoned railroad tracks not far from where we lived. By mid-evening, the temperature had dropped to the upper sixties but had remained dry. We wore shorts and tank tops; the goosebumps were visible on Anthony's suntanned arms. "Are you cold?" I asked as we walked toward the cemetery. "I'll warm you up!"

He laughed, "Not here, you won't!"

As we walked, we chatted about the bicentennial celebrations and his prospects for a summer job with the city. By nine that evening, the waxing gibbous moon was overhead. We entered the cemetery gate and strolled to our favorite spot. We saw no one, and we felt comfortable and safe. When the moon was right, bright beams streamed through the tall trees and illuminated the granite stones belonging to those underfoot. I could glimpse the slim-yet-muscled boy who stood naked beside me.

And as we lowered ourselves to lay upon our clothes, removed for the sake of flesh on flesh, the excitement within us rose in anticipation of what we were about to do. Almost immediately, the caresses and soft kisses began. Our limbs wrapped tightly around each other. Passions raged like fire. Within moments, the warmth from within exploded upon us simultaneously. We remained as we were for a long while, whispering our affections, talking of our history together, and avoiding the topic of what the future may hold.

Our place within the graveyard was our private haven, which embraced our capacity for simple musings and physical intimacy. It was tranquil and calm, shrouding and womb-like. The gravestones did not cry out or demand our attention. They were discreet and unpretentious, yet not without quiet significance. And we simply and easily coexisted with the granite and marble memorials.

But as we gathered ourselves to leave, Anthony became intrigued with the remains of our mausoleum. The structure was worn down by the soft hand of time.

"What is it, Ant?"

"I don't know. Something about it makes me think about my own death; it gives me a feeling of loneliness and sadness, you know? All these gravestones, this place… it's emotional. It has a spiritual richness, like they preach about in church, but it has a creepiness, too. The moonlight gives a mellow glow to everything. Underneath this ground is a different world, whispering. You can hear them, you know, if you listen hard enough with an open mind and a purity of thought. Strange, really. Don't you think?"

"I think you're being strange, and you're giving me the creeps, but if you say so, okay."

His reflection on the images around us forced me to contemplate my own mortality, which evoked loneliness and a tender sadness, just like he said. It also stirred a mingled bittersweet comfort. Yet his words eliminated that earlier tranquil and calm feeling. I had goosebumps on my arms, signaling that it was time to leave.

⁂

It was one of the last days of our summer jobs and a long, exhausting day for both of us. It was late when he called. I was to meet him at his house. His family was unexpectedly in Spencerport for a few days, for a family matter that he wasn't interested in discussing.

As hot as it was, it had rained all day. The streets were wet and shimmered under the streetlights. A breeze whispered through the trees, and rainwater sprinkled upon me as I walked to his house. It dripped down the back of my neck, under a T-shirt that did little to keep the weather off my skin.

The sunroom was stifling, and the overhead fan wasn't doing anything for us. We sat apart, tired and silent in our thoughts. He seemed a bit out of sorts. Eventually, I felt an unsettling mixture of frustration and pity. His demeanor was quiet, sullen. I wanted to be naked with him. Lay down on him. Feel him. Stroke his soft, tanned skin with my fingers. Discover his hard muscles beneath.

Slowly, as our silence drew out, his body moved closer to me, subtly leaning in, until finally, effortlessly, in the grace of a natural dance, his head fell lightly upon my shoulder. I could smell the heat coming off his skin. He was dotted with perspiration. I took in the sensual scent of his body. To be so close to him was a blessing that gave me peace. He sighed loudly and contentedly, his head almost nuzzling against my shoulder and neck. I put my arm around him and brought him in even closer. I was filled with a fierce desire, a need, to keep him safe from what troubled him.

Fall – Year Two

Labor Day 1976 crept up on us. The hours of sunlight slowly shrank. The air became cooler, bringing some reprieve from the oppressive heat.

Anthony's family was in Spencerport again for a family BBQ that Sunday, his grandmother included. He was agitated when I arrived; he had convinced his folks to leave him behind, so that we could ride back to the Adirondacks for the day, and his family's displeasure at his choice to stay was weighing heavily on him. From what Anthony had revealed, his grandmother had thought it unwise for him to remain at home. She may have had more influence over his parents and the household than I thought appropriate. Anthony was always close to his grandmother. But lately, they had been butting heads, and we both knew why. At the far end of the sunroom, stacked high, were the papers and books that I did not ask about. Beneath the uniform on the floor was a trumpet resting on its bell. The brass was sparkling in the sunlight. He noticed my gaze.

"I play the trumpet," he said. "Not that I want to. Another family expectation is that I learn an instrument. Jazz mostly."

Anyone, at any time, should be able to pursue or decline to pursue almost anything. But not for Anthony. Not yet, anyway. My only response was, "Oh. I didn't know."

Given our relationship, I must have looked disappointed for not knowing this about him. He explained, "We make it easy for the people we love, you know? We say it's okay. We tell ourselves it'll be all right when it isn't. We do what we can to keep them from hurting or feeling disappointed. To keep shame away. Even at the expense of our own happiness. It's family love. What can I tell you? We die so they can live happy with honor." At that, he gave himself a good laugh, but I didn't see the humor in it, and I didn't think he did either.

I dared to say, "I don't feel that way. My family —I love them, yes. But really? I'm an outsider to them. I know it. They may know it… or not. I don't care. It hasn't helped me. It reinforces my knowing that I am an outsider. Sacrifice me for them? Maybe before you. But not now. My life is yours now, Ant. It's what you allow it to be. It's what I had never expected it to be. But now my life is with you. Without you, there is nothing for me. It's not about what we do. It's about how I feel, what I have always hoped for but believed impossible. You are an addiction—a reason for me to get up in the morning. You know what it was like before us. You're why I continue to exist at all. I can't see life past you. I don't want to go back to just going through the motions of what my life was like. Not after this, us. I want to follow my heart now that I know what is possible and how it truly feels. I'll be eighteen soon. I'm not sure what that really does for me or us. But it must do something, yes?"

"Your lack of devotion to faith and family comes easy for you," he said. "But it doesn't upset me. My life crescendo is you."

"Crescendo? Music? I'm not a trumpet player, Anthony. I don't know what that means."

"Crescendo means at its peak, at its auditory crowning. I've achieved that with you. I don't know how or where we go from here. I'm trying to figure it out. If I can't figure it out, I can't go on. Remember the Catholic Catechism? Where they say, 'Heaven is the ultimate end and fulfillment of the deepest human longing.' You are my deepest human longing, my Heaven. I would consider the ultimate end to keep what we have."

"That's Catholic jargon, Ant. I don't know what that means. Can we not talk about this anymore?"

He sighed, and we didn't talk about it anymore. We buried our faces into one another. We inhaled each other. We relaxed into each other. We returned to the here and now, that which unburdened us of the tomorrow and beyond. We pretended that there was only now. But we both knew better. Tomorrow and beyond was coming.

At some point that day, we cruised north to the Adirondack foothills, where the cottage was. We just needed to get away. He wanted to return home from school next weekend to attend the Electric Light Orchestra concert at the Auditorium on Sunday, September 12th. The band Orleans was the opening act. He was grumpy, believing he had blown his chance of getting the okay from his parents after the conflict about the Spencerport family outing.

"My parents are on me about coming home from school so often. Academically, I did well. They complain that my last school year was spent mostly back home and not at campus. They don't understand why, and I can't explain it. I'm concerned my grandmother may betray me and us. I have got to be careful. I don't know what to do at this point."

The ride was a quiet one. The silence between us always brought an intimate sense of security, but today was different. It was as if we both needed to retreat to a dignified safety. I would learn however that safety was an illusion: it keeps the dangers of the world at arm's length, but only for so long. A blissful wait before the inevitable explosion. The explosion would come.

Anthony was not confrontational. For him to strike back at rules or push back when he was expected to be obedient and cooperative just wasn't him—it had never been him. He said he desired my presence in his life above all things, but he had apprehensions about family, faith, and us in the heart of it all. It was becoming clear that his pushback was worrying his family. Thanks to his grandmother, he was being questioned about my—"his friend's"—frequent visits. He was beyond troubled, and I had become relentlessly selfish when it came to us.

When we arrived, the woods were alive with sound in every direction: birds fluttering, dragonflies dive-bombing, branches clicking and leaves shivering as the wind stirred. Old pines, tall to the sky, groaned and rustled as they bent with the wind. A stream trickled nearby, squirrels chittering. It was as if autumn hadn't arrived here yet. We walked, explored, and enjoyed our time together, relaxed as we finally were. In my mind, I was coaxing the sun to shine on us as it broke through the trees.

We came across a lean-to in the woods, in an area that I had been familiar with since childhood. The well-built Boy Scout structure was made entirely of large logs, and it had been a mainstay in these woods for generations. It was impressively large, standing ten feet tall at its entrance, ten feet wide, and eight feet deep. We sat on a log that formed the opening of the structure, enjoying the ambient quiet of the woods. Little did I know then that it would be our last time experiencing the Adirondacks together.

Night had descended, and the air became cooler and drier. We sat tired and comfortable, silent in our thoughts, nursing a bottle of Chianti. We knew it was time to return home. An hour's drive would be welcomed; it would take up the time we needed to adjust to the restrictions we faced when back among the family members who governed our relationship. Being among the forested pines and the seclusion of the foothills allowed us to be who we were to one another.

"Let's go for one more walk before we head back."

"Okay," he said with some reluctance. "Night walking may be a little eerie here. Everything is black. No light whatsoever any-where."

"We'll be fine. I know the area well."

Night blanketed the landscape. It felt like a walk through the underworld. On this night, it was perfectly still at first: no wind, no birds, just the sound of our feet scuffing over a dirt-packed road. In the dark, any worries that I carry about returning home remain behind the darkness. I paused to look at the stars. He watches me. I've done it plenty with friends and family around a campfire, but nothing compares to tonight, alone with him. All those stars and all the possibilities that lie ahead, a stunning celestial show thanks to minimal light pollution.

"We often hear coyotes late at night here," I said. "Sometimes from deep in the woods, sometimes quite close."

"Should I be worried?" he laughed.

"Don't be scared when coyotes begin howling, and they will. You will be astonished by their wild calls and recognize how much our world intrudes on theirs."

"You know a lot about this place," he said.

I wrapped him tightly in my arms and kissed him before responding.

"I've spent quite a bit of time here, often alone. Not necessarily by choice, but it works for me. It can be magical here at night. The skies aren't as polluted with lights and such as you find back home. Here, you can see a remarkable display in the night sky. Sounds corny, I know. But in the Adirondacks, you get a front-row seat. Its dark skies make for some of the best stargazing."

I continued, "I would come to the Adirondacks in the fall when the leaves turned bright yellow, red, and orange against the bluest sky. In summer, it is cool here when it is hot everywhere else. And in spring, I could see things changing, the leaves unfurling, the ferns pushing themselves out of the dirt. Yeah, I know, it sounds dorky, but I've always loved it here."

There was also a meditative peace. But I didn't say that, although I hope he felt it too.

It was a quiet drive home, and that was okay.

❧

The months that followed had us back to our usual routine. Anthony would come home from campus often. He and I would continue our intimacy on those afternoons in the sunroom, his grandmother downstairs mostly, and Julia with friends until dinner time. Occasionally, we would take cold weather walks in the evening, rendezvousing nearby in the neighborhood. We often headed to the local cemetery, where we would have peace among the many who were no longer. It was when we were together that we were at our happiest. We talked of the lives we were leading when apart, the secrecy necessary to keep what we had safe, and the excitement of our next opportunity to come together again.

Sometimes, he was troubled by a row he had had with his family, regarding his frequent return trips from campus, his afternoon visitor (me), and his grandmother's insistence that he attend church with her. Over the past two years, we had learned how to negotiate the logistics of what we were doing. The fear of breaking social and religious norms had dissipated in me completely. They had not dissipated entirely in Anthony, however, but he had become wiser in negotiating our time together. Sometimes, his internal conflict would surface. We had to agree that all we had was the here and now, just to reel in his anxiety over what we had become and what would become of us.

༈

A few early-season snowflakes began to drift from the graying sky; he looked away from the window, sighed, and focused on me.

"Friday, October 23rd, is the Zappa concert in Buffalo. I was hoping to go to it with a group from campus. You should be able to come too, as it is not a school night. What do you think? My family wants me home that weekend, but if I can get away from that, I'd like us to go to the concert."

"Zappa is great getting high music! I would love to, but let's see how you manage not coming home that weekend," I replied. "I guess we'll see."

We were excited about the prospect of attending a public event together. The idea of crashing for the night in Buffalo and returning Saturday was exhilarating. But in the end, it turned out that Anthony was required to be home that weekend for a church function with family. The excitement of doing something away from home together was crushed. He didn't do well with the disappointment. It was one of the worst blows to his usual good cheer that I had noticed lately.

I couldn't shake the feeling that I was drawn to a part of him I suspected was deeply broken, something frightened and angry and hopeful all at the same time. But sometimes, a darkness would come over me, too. I wanted to say these sudden black moods had been happening only since us, but they'd descended on me for as long as I could remember, sometimes without reason or warning. But less so since him.

I would wonder for the millionth time if he would ever give me up. But he showed no sign of doing so. Instead, he would wrap himself around me like a guardian angel protecting me from harm. He talked me down when I stressed about keeping what we had safe and secure. He invented reasons to be cheerful, even when I knew he was sometimes troubled. He would hold me close to calm me when I worried about losing him to someone else. He would tell me that I was his dream come true, for what he had always hoped.

But he was troubled as well. I had begun noticing subtle changes in Anthony. Our time together, almost always pure bliss, had become more troubling for him. He had misgivings about our relationship and its consequences. He would torture himself, weighing the future and the possible regrets he and I may have one day. He seemed to lose more of his cheerfulness as he stressed about what his future, our future, would entail. On some days, he would express concern about his family and how they would feel, should he share with them his world as we knew it. Yet still, we had days where he was his tender and loving self. As time passed, our visits became fewer, and he appeared somber, brooding over what was to come. Ever affectionate, even when he was aching inside, his care for me and the warmth of his embrace never failed to come through, his tenderness never faltering.

I worried when he would contemplate the nature of our world and our place in it. I was forced to see the pain that he was in. I knew and felt that pain alongside him, too, but I was too young to realize the darker path that he was on. Though his thinking was often severe, he was always gentle with me. He worried about what our future would become, while I was delighted thinking about what our future could be. His feeling that everyone had abandoned him, even God, made him feel the most alone. He seemed worried about his sense of identity, self-worth, and relationship with God and family.

I didn't see it at the time and didn't know what he may have intended. When he spoke of these things, there was nothing impatient in his manner. Quite the opposite. The silence that followed should have been more worrisome to me. Looking back, it was as if it were perfectly understood, but it wasn't. I should have known the shadows were calling him. It was times like this, when he would speak of the future so hopelessly, that I was truly worried for him. I loved what I had found in him, in us. But I tried to reconcile his concerns, which seemed to be above my maturity level at the time, with the joy of having found him. I was young and innocent but with a bodily ache that drove me. In times like this, I wanted to touch him, not with a selfish outcome in mind but with an ache to make him feel better. When I put my arms around him and pressed my body to his, it was to satisfy my ache but also to ease his pain, pain that he was able to release while we were together.

"Just hold me," he would say. And I would.

We would embrace for a long time, never seen in public, impermissible; the same touch that would elicit disapproval and scorn... hidden from the eyes of others. It was times like this when he would suppose the future, when all the ease we had enjoyed together, would be gone. It would take away the safety I had felt with him; I hadn't realized that it could be dissolved so easily.

I was ignorant then of everything but my happiness; life just seemed magical. We were launching merrily down the path of sin. That was how his family would have seen it. But it had been two years. We had each other. Nothing else mattered.

I continued to immerse myself in our neighborhood social circle when Anthony was unavailable, and I didn't have to work. It was usually late afternoons during the week. Julia was almost always among us. She would inform me when Anthony was available or when he was away at school. It was strange that our arrangements to meet were often communicated by Julia. Anthony and I would plan our rendezvous when he was home for any length of time. As we were covert lovers, our approach was as exhilarating as it was somewhat silly. But it was before the rainbow, and flying the Pride flag was years away.

❦

It was a late November afternoon. The days felt fleeting, as if you had to hurry up and finish whatever you were in the midst of. Autumn is that waiting room before you enter winter's cold, dark chamber. I was with our small group, roaming the neighborhood.

"Anthony is home and hopes you'll come by," Julia whispered. "Our grandmother is visiting friends for the afternoon. He had tried calling but had no luck catching you at home."

The day was meant for rain. The afternoon was beginning to darken for the arrival of evening, which now came earlier and earlier each day. I was waiting on the porch after I softly rapped on the outside of the door. As he opened it, the dull afternoon light flowed across the dimly lit threshold, carrying moist air infused with the rich scents of late autumn. There was Anthony, smiling and offering his warm embrace. A smile from him could brighten up the darkest day. I followed his gesture and allowed my body to absorb the comfort and strength, giving my own to him in return. The embrace held a lifetime of longing.

"What are you doing home unexpectedly?" I asked.

"My dad is putting snow tires on my car before winter hits. Surprise! Let's walk."

"Let me stop at my car on the way." I had a bottle of Chianti to bring with us.

We stepped onto the leaf-covered sidewalk and made our way through the neighborhood. The streets were typical of hometowns like ours—neighborhoods of one- and two-family homes, small yards, big trees, and wooden fences. These were the houses and surroundings in which we grew up.

The fog was heavy—a typical November day. There was no moonlight or stars, not yet. He stared off into the distance, watching the darkening tree line. I couldn't see his face. I couldn't read his thoughts. We were at our place in the neighborhood cemetery, hidden behind the Burke and Allyn mausoleum under the great oak. Faded flowers and tiny American flags fluttered in the breeze—leftovers from the Veterans Day holiday.

"Why not at your house if your grandmother isn't home?" I asked when he shivered noticeably.

"She'll be home soon and then call for me to help her with this and that. Let my parents deal with it. They'll be home soon anyway."

It was completely dark now, and I had begun covering him with kisses and nibbling on his smooth body as he shivered. We took sips of Chianti from the bottle, and I promised that I and the wine would keep him warm. Nibbling on the inside of his hip caused him to giggle aloud, and I whispered, "Shhhh! Someone will hear us!"

"You know that tickles me," he laughed. "Wait. I have something to tell you, and I can't do it while you're chomping on me!"

I looked into his smiling eyes and wondered why he would want to interrupt my need to devour him.

"Okay, I'm listening." I wondered if it were good news or bad news that couldn't wait.

"My father says that if I continue to make these frequent trips back home, my car won't last, and he has no plans to replace it if it dies."

"Well, Ant. It is a '62 Biscayne. It wasn't built to last as long as it already has! Chevy stopped making that model for good reason. And those snow tires are probably worth more than the car."

"Yes, but how will I get home if it dies, and really, you're making fun of my car now?" he laughed.

"Shhhh!" I whispered. "I'll come to get you."

"Oh yeah, I can see myself trying to explain that to my family. My young friend comes to get me and brings me back to school just because he's a nice guy. That won't work."

"Tell them you took a bus."

"They'll ask where I get the money for frequent round-trip bus fares."

"Well, the truth is, Anthony, I need you in a way that I haven't needed anyone, ever. I crave you. I miss you like crazy when you're not here. I ache for you. I feel complete when I'm with you. Being wrapped up with you like this is all I can think of. It's all that I want. I won't be without you. I was always afraid that I was not meant for this world. And then came you. You know this! And now we may see less of each other? No!"

"Yes. I do know that. But that's a lot of pressure on me. We'll figure something out. I don't want to lose what we have, either. It's also all that I have, too."

At that, the topic of conversation was over. He wrapped himself around me, but my enthusiasm for why we were there had faded.

"I know you're upset," he said. "It'll be okay. Alright?"

"I hope so," was all I could say, realizing our time together may become less frequent. It already wasn't enough.

"Come on," he said. "We have time now. Let's just enjoy it."

I climbed inside his sweatshirt as he laid back on the cool, damp ground and I began nibbling on him again. His boy fragrance of youth and innocence quickly drove me out of my mind. His undone jeans slipped off easily as he pulled his sweatshirt off his body. Brisk as it was, he was very cooperative for someone who became chilled so quickly. And, as always, he let me have my way with him. The heat of our passion warmed our bodies despite the damp, cold November evening. It was all that I wanted, all that I needed. His good cheer for my performance was my reward for pleasing us both. I could never give this up. Could never give him up.

On our way home, he commented, "You were amazingly wild tonight."

"As I've said, you drive me crazy!"

"I think it was the wine," he laughed. "We need to have it with us more often!"

⁂

It was days later. The November sky was gray, and the forecast predicted the year's first snowfall. As a stiff, cold breeze blew, we walked beneath a canopy of leafless trees. He pulled the collar of his coat up higher around his neck and crossed his arms in front of his chest. I noticed he felt the chill, and I wanted to wrap my arms around him to keep the cold away. As we walked, a tree whose giant roots had pushed up the broken sidewalk reminded me of something he once said: 'Are we innocence destroyed? Sinners to be punished?' Were we broken like the sidewalk, not noticing what our roots may have been doing to us over the years? If we were broken, the roots of what caused the damage extended further back than I could see.

It began to snow heavily, and the falling flakes in the twilight were beautiful. But, like that broken sidewalk, no one noticed the quietly occurring damage. The innocence that was being destroyed.

Winter/Spring – Year Two/Three

It was a few days before Christmas, and we were not yet accustomed to the icy winter. He called me at home and asked me to meet him at the nearby corner. So, I did. He stood in the dark of night under a broken streetlight, bundled against the cold. We briskly walked the neighborhood, trying to stay warm. The penetrating chill wasn't helping. It was snowing hard, the kind of snow that settles on the ground and sticks. The snow on the road was slushy and dark from being driven through by cars, but it was far more than a few inches deep on either side of the road. We were quiet as we trekked through the snow and slush. It was as if the silence found the words for us when words weren't necessary. But then they came.

"I learned tonight that my grandfather's pension has been paying my tuition," Anthony said. "I got into a loud and terrible fight with my parents and grandmother. My grandmother was giving her opinion of what I should be doing post-graduation, and my parents were not defending my right to choose my own path, which I made clear I would be doing exactly that. I don't know if they were not pushing back because they respected her or were considering her opinion without my input. I just lost it. I lost it really bad, like never before. She brought up that my friend, you, may be distracting me from focusing on what's important, whatever the hell that may be. But she didn't go any further. I knew it was her way of holding over my head what she suspected."

He continued: "I don't care anymore what she suspects. She actually suggested that I meet with our parish priest for my outburst. My father's only response was for me to calm down. That's when I called you, hoping you would be home. And then I walked out. Such bullshit!"

Anthony added, "She wants me to see our priest—spend time with him, have him counsel me on my 'recent moodiness, disrespect, and defiance,' as she puts it. I believe she is holding us over my head. She has no idea what kind of person is hiding behind that church vestment. No idea," he said with such disdain.

"What do you mean?" I asked.

Tears lit up in his eyes, and he quickly turned his back to me.

Again, he whispered as if talking to himself, "She has no idea."

"Are you okay?" I asked.

"I'm fine, as long as I stay away from him," he responded, choking back a sob.

"Ant? Are you trying to tell me something? Did something happen?"

"No!"

"Has he ever hurt you, Anthony?"

"No. Just drop it, please?"

"Have you ever been alone with this priest, Anthony?"

"Please, just drop it. Please."

I saw that there was something undefinable buried inside him, a sadness of sorts that may have always been there... a vague reminiscence of something unpleasant, perhaps scary, returned to him.

Nothing concrete that I could decipher, just a blur of feeling. There was no seeing through to his thoughts.

I went to him and wrapped my arms around him, not caring who was around to see. I pulled him tightly to my chest as he trembled. He released a long, heavy sigh. He wiped his eyes. Then turned to me and said again, "Let it go, please. I'm fine."

And I did let it go… while with him. But I couldn't help thinking about the rumors and the jokes I'd heard from neighborhood peers over the years. Could it all have been true? There was a story buried in the creases of his trembling, but he asked that I let it go.

I saw in him such true innocence and the monstrous crime committed against him. We entered the cemetery and made our way to our mausoleum. He sat down and leaned back against it, as cold as it was. The ground was wet, and we shivered in the cold together. He shut his eyes and sat for five, ten, then thirty minutes. I could hear his soft, unconscious breaths as he rested. After a while, he opened his eyes and looked over at me.

The spirit can be as wounded as the body, and when these wounds do not heal, well… we struggle to find something to do, something to say at times like this. So, I said nothing and waited for him to speak.

"Warm me up," was all he said, and I did.

I showed him that I loved him, and he was most wonderful. He was defenseless in his world, and so I loved him—and hated his world—all the more.

Depressive episodes closed around him like curtains. They would hang there for weeks.

❦

The winter of 1976, transitioning into that of '77, was one of the worst winter seasons in upstate New York memory. Heavy Great Lakes snowstorms and severe blizzards continued all the way into spring. The cold was unprecedented. Worst of all was the blustery wind that would not quit. Wind chill temperatures often ranged far below zero over prolonged periods, which made the cold feel even colder. Lake-effect snow squalls paralyzed communities from the Great Lakes to eastern New York, and it wasn't unusual to get several inches of snow per hour.

Driving conditions were often so bad that Anthony was forbidden to come home in that weather. It was the first time we had seen each other so infrequently in two years. It was the most miserable period in our lives since we had met. It must have pleased his grandmother.

Spring had finally arrived. It had been a long and dreary winter, and for a while, it seemed like the sun would keep hiding forever behind the clouds. The weather the past few months had been terrible, with the frequent snowstorms and the strong winds. His trips coming home this past winter had been few and far between. He had missed coming for my birthday in March, which he felt bad about. But he knew coming home for that would complicate things with his family, and he knew he would have to be home again anyway for the upcoming Catholic holidays. We would find the time to rendezvous outside his home while much of the holiday and church commitments consumed most of his time.

It was cold that Good Friday evening in April before Easter. A stiff breeze blew through the trees and over the snow-covered ground on which we stood. He pulled the collar of his sweater up higher around his neck. He still felt chilled and decided to return to his house for a warm winter coat. I waited outside the front door when he went in. I noticed his grandmother peeking out the window. Moments later, he returned and appeared to be upset. I placed my hand on his shoulder, looking for an explanation. He gently pushed it away.

"Let's get out of here."

I nodded and followed him as he quickly left the family home.

The street was empty. The temperature had dropped, making the sidewalk slippery enough that we had to pay attention as we made our way in silence. His breath floated from his lips in tiny white clouds. His cheeks and nose were rosy, the dark blue color of his coat enhancing the pink hue on his skin. I couldn't help the smile that stretched across my face. I wanted to touch his face, lick his lips, feel the curve of his mouth with mine, taste him. But he was in a mood that was very uncharacteristic while we were together. It had been a long time since I'd seen him upset like this, and each time had to do with family or religion.

The branches of the trees brushed against each other in the cold wind, making a sound that reflected my cloudy thoughts. It was easy for me to get lost in my head… too easy, and rarely was it helpful. I worried about my only time with him this weekend, with him stressed about whatever had gone on at home when he had retrieved his winter coat. He seemed elsewhere.

The sky grew darker, the air cooler. He pulled his coat tighter around his body. Then, out it came.

"I don't know why I come home."

"What?" I responded, alarmed.

"No, no. Not you. You're why I come home at all these days. It's just that my time, my whereabouts, and my life get micromanaged when I'm home. I used to think they did so because they care, and they do, but when will they let go? Can't they just trust that I know what I'm doing? Know that I won't bring them trouble or shame? You know? Can't they just let me be? They don't get it, and I can't really explain it to them. Jesus, and my grandmother. Christ! They let her dominate my life like I'm her husband or something. Can't she just leave me alone?"

"Let's go to my car and warm up. We'll drive for a while." I had nothing else to say or offer. It was an area of grief for him, where I knew he wouldn't appreciate my thoughts on the matter, although he knew what they would be. He thought it was easy for me not to have family and faith commitments. He was envious, but he was wrong. I did. But I was selfish with what we had. And I was very protective of it. Of him. Yet he struggled.

We drove along the perimeter of the cemetery before entering. The streetlights emitted their yellow glow, and the night shimmered. I killed the headlights as we entered and the light faded, making it hard to see. The moon was half-full, but the sky was clear and the stars bright. It was cold that night. I knew we only had a little while before I needed to get him home. But I wanted the warmth of his face on mine, if only for a few minutes. I needed to breathe in his essence in the warmth of the car. I needed to taste his lips, if only to have something to hold on to until I saw him again. I needed to know that he would be okay when I returned him to his family and faith.

❦

It was late in the season, and the actual spring weather had finally arrived. It was a gorgeous day, maybe sixty degrees, with a cloudless sky that was so blue it looked almost navy. The contrast of the trees against the sky was beautiful. I was on my way to see him, and the realization of it all struck me suddenly. My life with him was beautiful. How was this possible when only two years earlier, my life held nothing to compare to this exhilaration, this bliss? It was as if something I had misplaced a lifetime ago was finally found. I felt an intense longing and desire for something lost, something that I had never had in the first place, but that my heart believed was mine.

Summer – Year Three

We often frequented our place in the local cemetery at night when we were home for the summer. We both had summer day jobs that neither of us was thrilled to have needed, and summer afternoons in the sunroom had become problematic. The graveyard grass was always freshly cut and emanated the season's scent. Fresh bouquets abounded, perfuming the night air. It was a mild summer evening, just after nightfall. It had been a hot day. The air was dry and comfortably warm. The night was moonless. The graveyard was black. Our bed, a thin layer of summer clothes no longer on our bodies, protected our skin from the grass. I could feel him, every bit of him. He emanated warmth from the golden glow of a suntan. His body was firm and hard. His fragrance was as natural as a craving. He allowed me to own him, a possession I would never willingly give up. I knew his body like my own. I understood how he felt and how he tasted. I knew all that was knowable to bring him to feel love and pleasure, and then to feel secure, warm, and relaxed. There was nothing I wouldn't have done to him, for him. He was the temple that I worshipped. He was my boy angel. My gratitude for his existence was indescribable. Our haven of love among the dead.

Gravestones—here, and everywhere else—record the passage of time, inscribing wind, rain, heat, and cold. Their language of discoloration, and other forms of attrition, is a testament to their history. They possess strength of character. They have no need for status or validation, and they welcomed us every time we came. Familiar sounds suggested the sad-beautiful feeling of death from ages ago: the cooing and caws of mourning doves and crows, and the forlorn ringing of distant church bells accented the air. The wail of sirens echoed through the streets of neighborhood homes. I should have sensed the omen that it all was, but in my bliss, it was not to be.

It was several days later, still early in the summer. The sky was a deep blue, and the sun, just topping the treetops in the late afternoon, burned off the clouds. The heat was paralyzing as I walked to his home. It burned on my skin, and the bright sunlight stung my eyes. He greeted me at the door. I entered, and we climbed the stairs to the sunroom. I could tell that something was different. His worry about us seemed to have dissipated. It was unbearably hot in the sunroom. The sweat ran down my face and neck. My jeans and T-shirt clung to my skin as I hurried to remove them, following his lead. It was too humid and sticky to be intimate. So, we lay beside each other, under a ceiling fan noisily wobbling overhead.

"Whatever happens, know that I love you," he said, his gentle eyes not leaving me.

I felt with my whole body that something had changed in him. A burden had fallen away from him, as if he expected nothing more from life. Not because he was disappointed or embittered. The crippling, all-consuming worry of what to do about us that would deplete him of all vigor was gone. No fear. Not even sorrow. It no longer chained him. He was free.

We lay quiet until I knew it was time to leave. It had cooled down some. He offered to walk with me to the car parked several blocks away. Whenever I looked at him, I couldn't help thinking of honey—maybe it was the gold tone of his skin, or his warm smile. He appeared to glow from within in the golden light of summer. In that diffused sun, which warmed but didn't burn in the late afternoon, its rays invigorating but never blinding, we enjoyed the neighborhood streets.

⁂

It was in early July. The air was thick and hot with moisture. We should have been celebrating his 22nd birthday. Several days passed, and there was no Julia, and I hadn't heard from Anthony. It was unusual that she would be missing from our social circle for any length of time. Anthony, being older, wasn't part of that same circle. Strange as it may have sounded, I didn't know if he had any social circle outside of his school campus.

Our group meandered the neighborhood as we had always done, our cars parked nearby as we loitered on one street corner or another. We would keep each other updated on our young lives, knowing that I could not share much of what the others enjoyed discussing. When a couple of days turned into several days without Julia being among us, I was beyond troubled, yet I couldn't share my concerns with the rest of the group. The uneasiness I felt was overwhelming.

It was early evening on a baking-hot, windless day. The leaves overhead held perfectly still. A breeze would have been nice, I was thinking. The sun would set soon, and the cloudless sky was painted a beautiful blend of red, orange, and violet. The sun's intensity suggested that the next day would also be sunny and hot. As I came upon the group, I still saw no Julia. I sensed that they had been talking in hushed yet dramatic whispers. And then it came.

"Julia's only brother died," a mutual friend among us said.

My insides immediately exploded with pain and twisted agony. I refused to believe it, but with the crippling pain that invaded my body, I knew it to be true. It was immediately followed by the shock that he had taken his own life, found hanging in the closet of the sunroom. I remember shouting, "It can't be true!" Heart-wrenching pain took over my body. At that very moment, I bolted to keep from falling to the ground and flailing about in agony.

Leaving my car behind, and as we were not far from where Anthony and Julia lived, I began running to their home. A sudden fever was boiling my flesh, the intense heat causing me to collapse. I struggled to my feet and stumbled away, not caring what my friends thought of my strange behavior, ignoring their calls to come back. My body felt inflamed, the sensation of pins and needles painfully piercing my flesh. I ran to his home, screaming, "Anthony, please, no! Please, no, God! Don't let it be true." Arriving at his home, my body shutting down from the agonizing possibility that he was gone, I sobbed violently, uncontrollably, not caring who would see. I stared at the sunroom through tear-filled eyes, pleading for him to look down at me, as he always did when I was expected. Clamping my teeth down, burying my face in my hands, squeezing my eyes shut, pleading that the rumors were untrue. My legs and arms painfully vibrated out of control. Electric currents ran through my body. The black manacle of grief closed around my shattered heart and locked into place like a horrible sickness. Then I knew.

I saw that the shades, yellow with age, were drawn in the sunroom, blocking any view into what was our room. The windows reflected the setting sun. I was a spectacle outside a home that had just experienced tragedy. With my head pounding, I willed my body to carry me away. The abandoned railroad tracks, just a city block from where I stood, with overgrown vegetation, provided me a place to retreat undetected and suffer the most excruciating pain I have ever experienced.

Hidden alone among the tall brush, I tried to make God have it not be true. I begged God to take me with him. I promised everything holy if He would put us together again—here in life or there in death. I wanted to be with him more than I wanted life itself. Suffering violent convulsions, my mind screaming in terror and grief, I prayed to God to make me lose consciousness, to die, to escape into nothingness where the pain couldn't reach me. I wanted to go be with him. Yelling with such bile, I cursed God for taking him and begged Him to take me too. I'd make a deal with the devil if God didn't come through for me, the God I did not believe existed.

My cursing God continued to burst from my throat between calls to Anthony to come back to me. Each wail wrenched the strength from my body. I willed my heart to stop, my lungs to cease, for death to come to me. I had lost complete control.

I must have been there for hours. I just don't know. I was completely drained of the will to go on. I knew I was alone with my grief. I knew I couldn't explain to anyone how I felt or why. I didn't believe that anyone would understand how I felt or that they would care. I would be carrying this agonizing grief alone for always.

Dusk had turned to night, the moon nearly full, glowing in the violet sky, and the first stars glimmered as they appeared. I must have lost consciousness. I had vomited on myself. My face was marked with tears, mucous, and grief as I raged that death hadn't come to me too.

I was truly alone, as I had always expected to be, before Anthony had given me a glimpse of what life could be like. I missed him so much. The light in his eyes, his low, soft voice, his tender lips, and the warmth of his embrace gave me hope that I, too, could be forever happy in this lifetime. But it wasn't to be. Alone again with my demons, the same demons he had banished from my world for so short a time, the same demons that would cause him to take his own life. I was eighteen and no longer a child. And yet, I knew nothing of what was to become of me. I cried more than I had in years. I was overwhelmed with a mixture of grief, guilt, and uncertainty that, in the end, he and I had done what love would have deemed to be right.

As Time Passed...

My grief went on for years without relief. Thinking about him would bring such horrible anguish that would never fully recede. The stabbing ache inside me would continue. The painful sensation of pins and needles in my flesh would surface repeatedly; I felt the need to stay mired in that foggy no man's land, like the moment between sleep and waking when a vivid dream slides away, one unlikely image at a time. The suffering of so great a loss would visit me for many years to come, and the conditions of our relationship would cause me to suffer entirely alone. I yearned for him for years and still miss him to this very day.

I tried to think of anything I could have done that would have changed the outcome. Grief is love with nowhere to go, and this unresolved grief is still mine alone. When it surfaces, as it does from time to time, it still numbs my spirit, breaks my heart, and drains my veins. Thinking about him sometimes overwhelms me with grief and immeasurable loss. Yet I must remain silent. When engulfed by the pain, it seems like my losing him was just yesterday.

Nothing in my life has changed me more than the love and loss of Anthony. It's a kind of forever pain that resides deep within me. It's suffering of the worst kind. No one else would know how I felt. Wanting Anthony to return was sometimes so intense that it stripped me of other desires. Life had no meaning; joy was out of bounds. My mind was filled with intrusive thoughts about death and uncontrollable bouts of sadness, guilt, and regret.

Buried in the neighborhood cemetery, there stands a simple family stone, the only thing left tangible of Anthony's existence. I'm drawn to this site every year during the first few days of July, the time of his birth and death. The religious concepts of the ever-lasting soul and life thereafter bear no significance to me. But I am drawn to his grave anyway. To talk to him. To ask him why. To wish him peace. To be reassured that he no longer has pain, and to be forgiven for not knowing, and to forgive him for leaving me back at that place where I was before him.

And then it starts again. The horrible vision of his last moments twisting up inside me, grieving a deeper hurt than anything ever sustained by the body. A wounded body heals itself, but there is a scar. The same must be true for the soul. It's the wounding of the soul that is still not healed. Sometimes, I still weep my heart out over my private sorrow from these visits, as if it were just yesterday when it happened.

I had many beautiful and tender memories, for which I am very thankful. But they couldn't answer the questions running through my mind. Everything that's been done to us we carry forever. We do our damnedest to hold on to the good and forget the rest. The worst is stored in our hearts, in a place our waking minds can't or won't touch.

Yes, the years have helped. Others have come and gone. Anthony was the sweetest first in many ways. Sometimes, I would see him in the blue quiet of the morning, or in the black hush of the night. He would be as he had always been. Sweet and pure. Warm and tender.

Young and beautiful. In the ebb of my life, the thought of him makes the years melt away. My love for him rekindles. My need for him begins to burn again. The loss renewed. A first love gone. And still, quietly, the suffering continues.

Section III

. . . and Other Stories

Nature's Gift:
Darkness in His World

Andrew's friend, born with nature's gift of same-sex attraction, had said odd things within what seemed like a normal conversation. Andrew noticed some unusualness but did not question his friend or think about the peculiarities of what was spoken. His friend died soon afterward.

Another of Andrew's friends, with the same gift of nature, had made strange comments of his own to Andrew, within what seemed to be in the context of a normal conversation. Again, Andrew had noticed some unusualness about the words, yet did not comment, question, or think about the peculiarities at the time. This friend, too, had died soon afterward.

Sometime later, upon learning of the deaths of his two friends, Andrew recalled and re-thought through the oddities spoken by the two: two people who once were one, within one world, yet apart and alone. He suddenly felt that he had become a stranger in a world he believed he knew and knew well, a world he thought was his own. He felt vulnerable, threatened, and inadequate. An obsessive self-examination of his life and the world around him had begun to preoccupy him—his thoughts, his relationships, and all those that touched his world. There was darkness in his world, a world suddenly strange and unfamiliar.

Yet another, also born with nature's gift, has passed. Andrew ventures out of the dimly lit funeral parlor and into the night air, crisp from the cold and dark, just as nature decided it would be. He wonders about the purpose of calling hours; what was viewing his dead friend all about? Why "calling hours?" His memories of his friend were so different from what he saw laying there in the sleep box of death, now surrounded by family, friends, and flowers. This was just one last momentary viewing, shortly before his friend entered the crypt of eternal peace, also cold and dark, just like the night. Did nature require the crypt of eternal peace to also be that way, just as it governs everything else?

The consequences of poor judgment—an error brought on by emotion, the pressures of passion, a choice not made but bequeathed at birth by nature itself—now brings on eternal peace? A gift of nature, as dark as it was; a gift that could not be celebrated and admired, like many of nature's other gifts, but was instead to be scorned and persecuted. Nights are as dark as nature requires them to be. If nature, Andrew thought, bequeaths the gift of same-sex attraction—of simply being physically and emotionally attracted to those who are similar—it should be a natural part of the world, just like the darkness of the night. Nature has the last say on all these matters. Yet, for those with nature's gift, only in the end was their eternal peace. Andrew found this thought paralyzing.

Night noises, typical of urban life and known to Andrew all too well, brought his mind back to where he had been standing, on the stoop outside the funeral parlor, his friend inside now resting in peace. Calling hours, he noticed, were drawing to a close. A backlit cloud, silhouetted by the moonlight, passed overhead. Beyond its place in the sky, sprinkled in the cold night air, were the stars, keeping with the patterns of Greek mythology and other constellations. The Greeks, Andrew thought, had time to ponder the stars. So why were he and his friends being hurried through life in the shadows, having to stay one step ahead of death? Nothing made sense anymore, he thought. Nothing made sense.

The Death of Jon and Carly

He was a beautiful male specimen. Small framed and lean. He had the muscles and the agility of an athlete. His facial bone structure was perfectly symmetrical. His green eyes were deep, like the green of fresh dew glinting in the sunlight. He had gentleness in his smile, full lips, a nose that was rounded, and a prominent jaw that was curved gracefully around. The strength of his neck showed in the twining cords of muscle that shaped his entire body—strong arms, bold thighs and calves, a firm chest, and a tight abdomen. His skin was smooth, fresh, and unblemished. The blessings of youth.

He was an Adonis in her eyes. It wasn't just the girls whom he moved. One look, and both guys and girls swooned at the sight of him. At twenty-one years of age, he was the epitome of young male perfection.

Slender with soft curves, she was the most astonishing girl he had ever met... easy to talk to and fun to be around. Her long brown hair framed the face of a goddess. Her skin was like silk. Her luscious lips, her perfect nose, her enchanting smile. She had safe, innocent eyes. That was the best way he could describe them. She had a rare and authentic beauty, and she was something in his eyes. Robust and real. He had to have her. His hidden darkness needed her.

His emotions were not easily hidden on his young face. Sometimes his pain was evident in his beautiful eyes, but her innocence caused her to look past that. She should have proceeded cautiously when his eyes showed his soul, but all she saw was beauty. He was an ocean of hopeless grief, but she was to learn this in time. As she looked into his eyes, she saw what she felt, a simple thing: passion. Passion filled the windows of his soul with the brightest fire. A fire from hell, she would later learn. But all she saw in them was that he would fight for her life to the last tear. He would not let the world break her, she was sure of it, and she felt safe with him. She clung to him with that passion that made them beautiful together—that forceful, driving passion of youth.

He would often garner the attention of others. When girls would flirt with him, it was difficult for her. When guys showed him interest, he became furious, unreasonably so. She didn't understand that. *Why wasn't he as flattered?* she wondered. She should have given more thought to his quick temper, his fierce anger. But he was charming, fun, and attentive. Oh, so attentive.

They became lovers instantly, and she moved in with him too quickly. He had her hooked—a real charmer, and she knew it. He was a rebel, and life became fast and exciting. Parties, dancing, drinking, and then more drinking. His male friends were always in his company.

When he got his dream job as a police officer, he proposed marriage, and she accepted. They moved to the seclusion of the Vermont wilderness. Hilltop farms, peaceful lakes, stunning sunsets. Bright spring and summer mornings, the lush green broken by white church steeples appearing out of gentle valleys.

They rented a cottage far from other homes, stores, and life as she once knew it. Hidden in a forest of tall pines and silver maples, the little gray cottage had two windows in each of its four rooms. The windows were dressed in black shutters that matched the front door. The dated furnishings were particularly neat and clean. The cottage appeared to have been unoccupied for some time. Jon learned of it from a fellow officer.

Waking up in Vermont felt surreal for Carly. Her life with Jon was dreamlike in their fairytale home, luminous leaves falling like dancing raindrops, a magical story shining down upon her.

A wonderful serenity had taken possession of Carly's young soul, and sweet mornings of spring warmed her heart. Often left alone due to Jon's long hours on patrol, she still felt the charm of existence in this wilderness. It seemed created for the bliss of young lovers. Carly was happily absorbed in the exquisite sense of mere tranquil existence. The church, the local school, the general store, and the post office, often the centers of activity, remained at a distance.

But when his drinking didn't stop, her hell began. Blinded by her youthful innocence, she hadn't seen it coming. He was truly troubled but shared nothing of it with her. Whatever terrible secrets he may have had were like poison eating away at him. She knew nothing of them.

He became painfully lonely, even with her by his side. His drinking, his anger, and his violent episodes slowly escalated. His barbaric and undignified anger was masking fear, hurt, and shame in his young life. He would conceal from her the pain of his loneliness. He needed to hide some vulnerability, tuck away some ugliness, and cover up scars as if they were repulsive. Childlike in her once-fairytale love story, Carly was ill-equipped to understand his suffering, much less help him. He once believed Carly was that magic carpet that would take him away from all that troubled him. He thought he had found in her what he needed. But the magic carpet quickly unraveled.

As he often did, he arrived home for lunch during one of his patrols to check up on her. He had been drinking; she could tell.

"The alcohol, Jon," she said. "You're working! What are you thinking?"

He hauled off and hit her, closed fist.

"It's not your business," he yelled.

That evening when he arrived home after his shift, he was remorseful.

"Things will be different," he said. "I won't drink, and I won't ever hurt you again. I promise. Please?"

He sounded believable, she thought, sweet and sincere. Things improved, and she remembered what had attracted her to him. Days later, he came home from his shift drunk again, and after arguing, he punched her in the stomach. The next day, she gave him an ultimatum.

"Your drinking, or me. I can't do this anymore with your drinking."

He chose her. She remained. She needed to feel safe again.

But the drinking continued, and the abuse continued. She stayed, as she could not see a way out. She felt committed to the relationship. During brief occasions when he was sober, things seemed pleasant. This was when she loved him most. But her way of life soon became learning to hide the bruises. Jon wasn't good at leaving them where they couldn't be seen. *Was this intentional?* she wondered.

Sometimes, when Jon would come home after a longer-than-usual shift, he would have the scent of a man's cologne on his clothes, a cologne that was not his. On those nights, he would sleep in the second bedroom of their cottage. Often moody, he would reject her affection and push her away. Though Carly would be alone many days and nights, her need to have Jon close to her when he wasn't working seemed to anger him. He found reasons to push her aside and reject her touching him. Carly's simple sweetness and kind gestures toward him would often get repudiated with sarcasm and hostility.

There had been a time when Jon had insisted on spending time with her in clubs and bars, and his male friends were always by his side. Now he kept her isolated and alone. When not working, he spent his time in self-imposed isolation at home or out on his own, often for long hours into the night. He was inconsistent with his affection toward her. Sometimes he treated her like his living love letter, but her tenderness toward him often repulsed him. Jon would be sure to bring her back from the edge of feeling unwanted, in fear that she would leave. But he kept her at a distance, brooding quietly on his own.

Carly would sometimes think she had done something wrong, but she realized she probably didn't. He may have been confused about his feelings for her, even in denial. He didn't reveal anything to her; she saw his emotions as irrational. She saw his delight when he would run into a male friend or coworker while out. She would encourage it, since he was much happier when socializing with his male companions. But she didn't understand his need to isolate. She wondered where he could go for so many hours in these isolated surroundings, always coming home angry and wanting to be left alone.

His mood swings became severe and frequent. He would suddenly become cold and avoid her for weeks. There would be a period of friendliness and affection still short of intimacy. Their sex life had ceased entirely. He was always too tired or needed to go somewhere. Jon led her to believe he no longer trusted her to be his alone.

She remembered when he had been so considerate, kind, and overly friendly. After moving to the cottage, he had started to accuse her of cheating on him. He would call to check up on her, as if she couldn't be trusted in this remote wilderness. This wilderness became a hide-out amid the red-painted barns, winding dirt roads, rolling hills, and lush green valleys. A hide-out buried in mist after a rainstorm, once beautiful, now lonely.

How could I be cheating on him? she thought. She no longer had a car to leave the cottage, and she realized the mistake of being away from family and friends. Carly was isolated, which was his doing, and she no longer felt safe.

One day, he came home for lunch like usual during one of his patrols. He had already been drinking, drinking heavily. They argued. She went to sit in the yard behind the cottage on an old, decaying tree stump, covered in moss and damp from the morning rain. She'd done this in the past: bask in the sun and enjoy cool Vermont breezes during her lonely times. She found peace on this old stump, her go-to place when things got rough. Wildlife, including owls, turkeys, and deer, often visited her as they meandered past.

He hollered for her. She didn't respond. He put his fist through the back-door window. Glass crashed down everywhere. He came bellowing over, stumbling in the process. He reached her and dragged her back through the door and into the cottage. She then took a punch to the face. Then another, her perfectly beautiful face. She could hear and feel the cartilage in her nose crushing, the pain excruciating.

She broke from his grip, her T-shirt torn in the process. She ran out the back door and into the woodland. She hid behind a large Vermont silver maple, which was wide enough to hide her from Jon's view entirely. He angrily called for her to return. Still, she hid and waited for him to go back to work. She shivered in the dampness from the fear. She took in that earthy smell that rises after a light summer rain, that mysterious scent of organic decay in Vermont's wilderness, which lingered around moist soil. It had begun to soothe her. The tension in her body eased.

When he did finally leave, and she was sure of it, she returned to the cottage. She had blood dripping from her nose and immense pain in her eye. She tended to her scrapes and bruises, but what hurt her most was that it had happened again.

What will happen when he gets home? she had wondered. *Will he tell me that he is sorry again? Will he remind me that he isn't always like this? Will he blame me for antagonizing him? Will he say, I'm sorry, but... as he often does to avoid responsibility for hurting me? Will he start by saying, you make me so angry?*

She thought, *why would he want to be with me if I made him so mad?*

She cracked another ice tray with a twist of the wrist, the same wrist that had taken several blows as she had tried to protect herself from his punches. She let out a soft cry of pain. Her bruised eye throbbed and stung with every facial movement. She tightened her lips and felt anger, betrayal, and pain. She bit her lips, felt the anxiety and fear, and the pain surged. She again placed fresh ice cubes within a face cloth and wrapped them tightly.

She replayed every moment that had brought her to this point. She used the cold compress, ice-filled and tightly bound, to ease the pain she felt from the punches to her face. But the pain intensified, causing her to cry. *Here we go again*, she thought.

With her phone, she Googled what to do when suffering a blow to the eye. *Apply a cold compress*, she read, *but don't put pressure on the eye. If you need it, take over-the-counter acetaminophen (Tylenol) or ibuprofen (Advil, Motrin) for pain. See a doctor immediately if bruising, bleeding, a change in vision occur, or if it hurts when your eye moves.*

Her eye was swollen and closed. She couldn't see a doctor. She no longer had her vehicle, and she didn't understand why she had let that happen. Besides, the doctor would be required to report it. She knew this. And she couldn't call her dad. Not then. He had warned her that this might happen and that she should leave him. She didn't want him to know that it had happened again. She didn't want her dad to see her with an eye that was black, blue, red, and swollen shut. There was no telling what her dad would have done if he had found out. And worse, there's no telling what Jon would have done if he found out that she told anyone of the abuse. He threatened to kill himself if she did. He threatened to kill her if she did.

She had no family or friends to call for help or support in that remote Vermont wilderness. She couldn't reach the police because it could be Jon who would respond to the call. There were no over-the-counter meds in the house, and she didn't understand why that was. She could only apply a cold compress. The only help available to her... ice, face cloth, and tears.

When her phone rang, she knew it was Jon. She knew without having to look, as the ringtone she had programmed for him was the song "Love of a Lifetime" by Firehouse. If she answered the call, he would have thought everything was okay.

She didn't answer the call. She feared that he would come home during one of his patrols. She didn't know what to do. Her body trembled with fear. She was stuck, and when she realized that fact, it caused her to lose her breath and faint. As she crumbled to the floor, her cold compress dropped from her hand, and ice spilled beside her. She was still in the same T-shirt, bloodied from her nose, torn from his grip. The phone stopped ringing as it slid across the floor.

She didn't know how long she had been out when she was startled back to consciousness by a continuous knocking on the front door. She wasn't entirely sure what that sound was. The knocking continued, and she remained still. She became certain, confident, that there was someone at the door. She couldn't answer it in her condition. She looked like she felt: beat up, bloodied, and in pain.

They'll go away, she thought. She knew no one out there in those backwoods. She was miles from any home, business, or civilization. She didn't hear a vehicle pull up. She waited.

When the knocking stopped, she waited a few moments before getting up. She peeked out from the kitchen window using the one eye still capable of seeing. The window treatment, printed with a pattern of red barns and green pastures, kept her mostly out of sight from the outside. She saw no one.

Quietly, she moved to the front door. As she peeked out from behind the torn shade, she could see a folded flyer, a brochure of some kind, wedged into the storm door grill. She opened the door as she looked about to be sure no one was there. The storm door's window glass was gone, smashed by an earlier violent episode with Jon. As she reached for the brochure, she checked again and saw that no one was around. She snatched it, closed the door, and felt relieved that her abuse was still their secret.

As she opened the flyer and read, she gasped for breath and almost fainted on the floor again. But she caught herself, using the corner of the wooden stand by the front door, the same wooden stand where Jon would drop his gun and badge when he came home. The headline on the flyer hit her cold and hard. Their secret was no longer their secret. Someone knew. And she panicked. *What if Jon were to find out?* she worried frantically.

The flyer read...

Domestic Violence:
What to do if you are being abused.

First, know that you deserve better; this isn't your fault. If you're in an emergency, call 911.

It can be hard to decide whether to stay or leave. That's why it may help to start with a call to the National Domestic Violence Hotline at 1-800-799-SAFE (1-800-799-7233). Call from a friend's house or somewhere else where you feel safe.

You can also turn to friends, family, neighbors, your doctor, or your spiritual community.

Also, make sure you have an emergency escape plan:

Hide a set of car keys.

Pack a bag with keys, extra clothes, important papers, money, and medicines. You might keep it at a friend's house.

Have a plan for calling the police in an emergency. You might have a code word, so your kids, family, friends, or co-workers know you're in danger.

Know where you'll go and how you'll get there.

A friend

But who? She knew no one out there. Her family was several hours away. And they had never been there before. They didn't even know the address. Her mail came to a P.O. box that Jon had established, and he was the one who retrieved it when he was in town. She stayed in touch with her mom and dad by cell phone, email, and text messages. *So, who?* she wondered.

Back in the canary yellow kitchen of the cottage, she placed the flyer on the kitchen's gray Formica tabletop. She was sure she had always covered up the bruises, the bleeding, and the abuse. *Who would know?* she wondered. *Was the flyer placed there randomly by some organization going door to door?* She didn't know. And not knowing was bringing her fear… fear that Jon would find out. Fear that he would think she had told someone. Fear that he would accuse her of being in contact with someone in the community. Fear that he would make good on his promises, to kill her or to die.

Her phone rang. It was on the floor where it had fallen away from her when she had fainted. She reached for it and saw that it was her father calling. She hesitated, wondering whether she should answer it or let it go to voicemail. It rang and rang. She answered.

"Hello," she whispered.

"Hey Carly. It's Dad. How are you doing?"

"I'm fine, Dad. Why do you ask?"

"Geez, Carly. No reason. I just wanted to check in on you. We haven't heard from you in a while, so I wondered how you were doing. Figured you were busy."

"Yes, Dad. I mean, no, Dad. I mean, uh, yes, I've been busy. You know… a lot on my plate. But I'm doing okay."

"Are you sure? Something wrong? I'm calling because I just had this uneasy feeling. Do you need me to come out? I can be there in a few hours."

"No, no, Dad. No need to come out. I'm okay, just busy. You understand. Soon, though."

Her voice quivered, and she knew it. She only hoped that her dad wouldn't notice. The last thing she needed was for her father to see her how she was. Jon would be beside himself if she allowed that to happen. She didn't need that. She needed time to think things through, to figure out what to do.

"Honey, are you sure?" he asked.

"Yes, Dad. Please. Don't come out. I'll see you soon. Jon will be home any moment, so I should go. Give Mom my love. Talk soon. I got to go."

"Carly—"

She hung up. As she put the phone down, Jon walked into the house. She hadn't heard him pull up to the front yard as she always did. He looked upset. Really upset.

"Who was that you were talking to?" he asked.

"My father," she responded.

"Why did you feel the need to call him?" he shouted. "Crying to your daddy because you're useless to your fiancé!"

"No, Jon. He called me to say hello. I didn't tell him anything. He can call me if he wants. Why is that a problem?" She caught herself. She didn't want him to become any angrier than he appeared to be.

That was when he noticed the flyer on the kitchen table.

"What's this?" He picked up the flyer.

As he read, his face became flushed. The muscles in his neck and forehead tightened. He was about to explode, a look she knew all too well.

"What have you done?" he screamed. "What is this?"

He was still wearing his uniform, his badge, and his gun. As he crumpled up the flyer in his left hand, he reached for her with his right, his face twisted in anger. She could smell his drinking as he grabbed her by the throat. He slammed her against the wall, still gripping her throat, which kept her from being able to say anything—or breathe.

She tried to scream but couldn't. She tried to tell him no. She frantically tried shaking her head and mouthing, Jon, no! But she was unable to get through to him.

As he tightened his grip around her throat, he shoved the crumpled flyer into her face, hollering, "What did you do? What did you do?" Carly was losing consciousness. She was gasping for breath. Her eyes closed.

"Look at me!" he hollered. "Answer!"

His grip tightened. It was not long before Carly lost consciousness. After another moment or two, Jon released his grasp, and she slid down the wall to the floor. He kicked her, screamed at her, "Bitch, bitch, get up, you bitch! Look what you made me do!"

She didn't move. She would never regain consciousness.

Her beautiful Jon spit angrily, face flushed red, muscles in his neck tensed enough to explode. He knew what he needed to do next. He picked up the crumpled flyer, walked to one of the vintage red, vinyl-covered chairs, and sat. As he read the brochure, he reached for his duty weapon. He pulled it out of the holster, disengaged the safety, and cried uncontrollably. As the tears flowed and the mucus from his nose poured, he lifted his duty weapon's barrel and placed it under his chin.

"You were meant for me," he whispered.

It only took one pull of the trigger, and he slumped from the chair onto the floor. As the blood left his mortal wound, it flowed rich and red and puddled around Carly's lifeless body.

All she had seen when they met was that he would fight for her life to the very last tear. He would not let the world break her, she was sure of it, and she had felt safe with him. She had clung to him with a passion that made them beautiful together—that forceful, driving passion of youth.

Their fairytale beginning and tragic ending is not a story to pass on. It is a sad story, many-layered, and at the center of it was a girl trapped in an evil nest with a boy and his inner demons.

Storms on the Horizon

Together,
we have weathered many a storm.

We can, in some cases, call those storms adventures,
when we were much younger,
much stronger,
more caring.

There appears to be more storms on the horizon.

Some quite severe.

Can we weather those storms as well?

Or will those storms batter us
into non-existence?

Will we allow the tempests to separate us
into our individual havens,
as if we were never
together?

Or are we still able to find shelter
within each other?

Are we just too tired,
unlike when we were younger,
stronger,
more caring?

Those storms on the horizon…

I Shall Implode

Some things are just not *ink and paper* noteworthy. But many things are. Too often, they are thoughts that are simply too much to contain in the mind without sharing, yet too dark in the soul to expose, no matter what form of communication is used to express them. To do so would demonstrate a lack of wisdom and prudence. So, what are the options? Go mad? Write symbolically or in prose? Or in myth and impressionism?

Shall I write using all the colors of autumn, avoiding the use of non-descriptive black on white, issues often blurred in judgment by the gray which separates right from wrong? And what of those things that are purple in color? Those things from the bowels of my soul which all too often rise to the surface and create turmoil in the forefront of my mind? How shall I write of those things?

And what should I do of things that are more crimson in color and evil in nature? How do I unburden myself of those thoughts and memories and experiences without revealing their true meaning? If I am reduced to using black and white and sometimes gray, then what? Compromise the integrity of that which is contained in my mind's eye or in the depths of my soul? Will I go mad or go under and implode? Or risk it all and write it all? Shall I write with

all the colors of nature as I should or simply scribe in black and
white and gray?

    I believe…   I shall implode.

In the Spirit of Playmates

This feeling of greatness and joy once bewildered me, for the skies were gray and the air was cool. The dampness and wind did not sour my feelings of happiness and warmth. Though the benches were empty, and the buildings were dark, I did not feel alone or without light. The pavement, where all paths meet, was wet and cold, but the abandoned circle held no feelings of gloom. The white-faced clock stood high to the east, expressing new hope as time went on. It was dark and rainy outside with a lazy mist hanging low, but inside I felt the sunshine, warmth, and vibrational energy radiating from within. This wonderful emotion brightens this circle and its gloomy, dull aura each time.

The possibility of her being a ghost stayed at the back of my mind. I was not even aware of the presence of the idea, until one day in the circle of the schoolyard, where all paths meet, it became the cause of a quarrel between us, her and me. It was the only real quarrel we ever had.

It happened as we were beginning to build our imaginary playhouse among the benches where we would live and play as children forever. We sat in the shadows of the clock tower where we had first met and once played when life allowed. Upon our morbid departure, I thought all was lost, until we were brought back together to the circle where all paths meet. I was directing the general construction of our imaginary home, while she did the pulling together of details—wall colors, decorations, and what the panoramic views from our imaginary windows would display to us as we pretended to gaze out in awe and amazement.

As she worked our house into a home, she was singing to herself from hymns and songs and ballads. Now, as she continued to hum and murmur under her breath, it occurred to me it was she who had returned!

Suddenly, I blurted out before I could help myself, "What is it like to be a ghost?"

She stopped singing at once, and she looked at me slyly over her shoulder and laughed. But I repeated, "What is it like to be a ghost?"

"Like?" she replied. She turned fully to face me and laid a hand upon my knee, and she looked eagerly into my face. "Ah, you tell me!" For a moment, I did not understand her. Then I jumped to my feet and shouted, "I'm not a ghost!"

"Don't be silly, you," she said. "You forget that I saw you go right through the schoolyard gate when it was shut!"

"That proves what I say!" I said. "I'm not a ghost, but the schoolyard gate is, and that was why I could go right through it. The gate is a ghost, and the schoolyard is a ghost, and so are you, too!"

"Indeed, I am not; you are!"

We were glaring at each other now; she was trembling. "You're a silly little boy!" she said.

I thought resentfully that she seemed to have been growing up a good deal too much lately.

"And you make a silly little ghost!" she said. "Why do you think you wear those clothes and in that way? Such flowing, black clothes can't belong to living children I know! Such clothes!"

"These are my sleeping clothes," I said, indignantly, "my best presentable, sleeping clothes! I lie asleep in them."

"And you go about so, always in your sleeping clothes?" she asked scornfully. "And it is the fashion nowadays, is it, to wear only one slipper?"

"This is my sleeping slipper," I explained. "My other slipper had been left to prop the lid of my sleep box."

"Really, you are silly to give such excuses! You wear strange clothes that no one wears living because you are a ghost! Why I'm the only one in the schoolyard who sees you! I can see a ghost!"

She would never believe the real explanation of my clothes, and I chose what I thought was a shorter argument: "Do you know that I could put my hand right through you—now—just as if you weren't there?"

She laughed.

"I could!" I shouted. She pointed at me. "You're a ghost!" she insisted, laughing.

In a passion, I hit her with a blow upon the outstretched wrist. There was great force of will, as well as of muscle, behind the blow, and my hand went right through—not quite as through thin air, for I felt something, but more than it could have if she were living, as I suspected! She snatched back her wrist and nursed it in her other hand. She looked as if she might cry, but that could not have been for any pain, for the sensation had not been strong enough. In a wild defense of herself, she still goaded at me: "Your hand didn't go through my wrist; my wrist went through your hand! You are a ghost with a cruel, ghostly hand!"

"Do you hear me?" I shouted. "You're a ghost, and I proved it! You're dead and gone and a ghost!"

There was a quietness then, in which a mourning dove's cooing could be heard coming from the school buildings beyond the schoolyard. It was here at the circle where all paths meet, in the schoolyard, in the shadows of the clock tower. Here we once played, and here, we played again.

And then, I heard the sound of her beginning to softly weep. "I'm not dead!" she cried. "Oh, please, I'm not dead!"

Now that the shouting had stopped, I was not sure of the truth. I was only sure that she was crying, as I had never seen her cry since she had been a very little girl, wearing mourning black and weeping her way along the path to the circle where all paths meet—weeping for a death which came so early.

I put my arm around her: "All right, then. You're not a ghost. I take it back—all of it. Don't cry!"

I calmed her, and she reconciled at last to dry her tears and go back to decorating our imaginary house, only sniffling occasionally.

I did not reopen the subject that had upset her so deeply, although I felt that I owed it to myself to say, sometime later, "Mind you, I'm not a ghost either!" This, by her silence, she seemed to allow. And as our playtime ended, our departure seemed final, as if we were given this one last playtime to come to terms with what life had once allowed and death had now taken.

So, how is it that the sun is shining, and the young are smiling, and the day seems cheerful where all paths meet? When on the inside, the sun doesn't shine, the smiles are gone, and the feeling is not cheer, but empty and gloom. The white-faced clock with its cold black hands stands tall to the heavens, telling its passersby that time moves on quickly. But the passing of each moment is painful and heartbreaking. The benches are filled with the chattering of life's young, sitting under trees that shade them from the sun. But the shade is a shroud, as one child is missing, no longer to be found in the shadows of the buildings and along the sunny walkways. Many are here, in the circle, where all paths meet, but the one I long for will never visit this place again.

Brian

My new teaching experience included an eleventh-grade American History/Government class in suburban America. The school's student body was predominantly white, well-off, and far removed from diversity, in both concept and practice. It was here that I experienced this nearly invisible student. I am haunted by the experience, and I vow to find a way to bring peace to it.

But how? By rethinking the circumstances and considering all that I may have done wrong or neglected to do at all? What could I have done? What should I have done? Inexperienced as I may have been, there must have been alternatives to the approach I was trained to follow. But what were they?

Brian was a ghost, an almost invisible student. He did not appear to fit in with the mostly white, preppy peers with whom he shared a classroom. His dark, not always clean, hair was a bit longer than that of his peers, and his skin was darker than most others but not tanned. He had smooth skin, not plagued by the acne many of his fellow students had. His clothes were not of the designer brands he would see on others around him. He had long eyelashes, piercing black eyes, a full face, and a small frame.

He didn't carry a book bag like so many others. He carried a single notebook, but he seldom had something to write with. I never saw him smile; he never looked at me or anyone. His head was always hanging low, even when speaking or being spoken to. He would sit against the wall toward the back of the room and away from the body of the class. He never raised his hand, never caused trouble, never disrupted, never talked, and eventually he disappeared. The other students did not notice this apparition when he had appeared, and none of them had noticed that he was gone.

At the start of the school year, Brian quietly vegetated deep under a baseball cap that succeeded in hiding much of his head and face. After a few weeks, I realized that he had yet to submit a single assignment. I checked his notebook. It was blank. Not even doodling. I remember the first time I gave an assignment: a brief, in-class essay on the book, A Day in Your Summer—History in the Making. He asked for extra time because he said he couldn't write in class. He never turned in the assignment. He shrugged his shoulders and showed me a blank notebook each time I reviewed completed assignments from everyone in the class. When I would point to the blank notebook and ask him to write something, he'd often say, with complete sincerity, "I thought I had."

Homework and reading assignments I could understand, but how could he have been present and still miss all the worksheets we did in class? I counted the assignments when I collected them, and I should have noticed if his had been missing. I checked everywhere to ensure I hadn't misplaced any of Brian's work, but I didn't have a single piece of paper with his name on it; there was no evidence that he existed. I then remembered that with the collection of assignments, there would sometimes be a blank sheet of paper with no name on it. I recalled a few times when I reminded him of an overdue assignment. Each time, he had nodded in agreement but had never produced the work. When I would ask him for it, he either said, "I forgot. It's in my locker," or "I'll bring it tomorrow."

Well, tomorrows came and went, and Brian turned in no assignments. As I kept Tim—my supervising mentor teacher—informed, he would occasionally speak with Brian in ways and in words that only he and Brian would ever know. Tim assured me it wasn't me, certainly not him, and that Brian would eventually become a casualty of that all-too-wide crack in the system. Discussions with Brian proved fruitless. Tim's approach and advice were predictable.

Brian would become the first notch in my grade book, reflecting a casualty on the battleground of education. But how did Tim know of the outcome so early in the situation? Was it experience? Or was it possible that his sometimes-cavalier approach to these situations and the Brians of his career contributed to the outcome? Tim would often refer to it as "seasoned cynicism."

In the end, less than three months into the school year, Brian stopped coming to school. Sometime later, when the notice came that he would not be returning, Tim declared it my first casualty in a way that he seemed to find humorous. He was lighthearted about it, although his explanation for why Brian was lost did seem to make sense but was not sensible. Tim was, apparently, unaffected.

I, on the other hand, was just short of devastated. Here was a student who, for the better part of several months, had almost no existence, no proof that he was once a student in my class. There was an apparition of a boy who had since disappeared, and as far as I can tell, none of his peers had even noticed that he was gone. If he ceased to exist altogether, would he even be missed? Would there be any evidence that he had existed at all? Had he contemplated these same questions in his mind? It would be awful to think that a sixteen-year-old child may have such thoughts. Maybe worse, here I was, his teacher, inexperienced and probably incapable of being that influence he may have needed to make a difference in his life, however small.

I'm sorry, Brian. I wasn't ready for you.

And I have yet to bring peace to this haunting experience.

The Joy of Ironing

It was a beautiful sunny Saturday, and I was grounded for some reason, which happened a lot those days. A dirty look. A smart-ass remark.

A warm breeze flowed through the house, mixing with the sweet, floral scent of dryer sheets. The sound of my peers at play trickled in from the neighboring yards, torturing me while I was trapped indoors. Strange the things you remember when recalling nothing of importance. Nothing earth-shattering. Just the ordinary. Ironing clothes is of the ordinary.

There was a console TV in the living room, like a piece of furniture. It was not turned on. Upon it rested a replica of the Pieta, a representation of the Virgin Mary, with Christ held on her lap. Christ looked like he was napping in her arms.

Also in the living room was Mom, lying on the family sofa, looking to take a midday nap herself. That was when my anxiety surged. Everyone's anxiety surged when she went lateral on the sofa. She insisted that life and all its noises cease completely so that she could nap undisturbed. The violent diatribe that she would dole out when her naps were disturbed would be harsh. Brutal, even.

Before she dozed off—before she even closed her eyes—I dared to tell her that I was *bored*. I was not sure why I said it to her, of all people, but it was true. I was also not sure where my siblings had disappeared to. They likely went into hiding because Mom was going down for a nap. If I had not been trapped, I would have also made my way to being invisible. Of course, she must nap in the middle of the living room, where life and all its noise take place for this family of ours.

A basket of clothes sat by the sofa, fresh out of the clothes dryer. They were forming wrinkles as they sat in the basket. The iron and ironing board were set up next to the sofa. Napping was her alternative to ironing clothes. She would have had someone else do the ironing anyway, as she often claimed to be too tired. She always had a reason to get a nap in, painful as it was for the rest of us.

"Iron clothes if you're bored," she snapped.

And now that she had said *iron clothes*, I was stuck having to iron clothes. It would not have been a good idea to walk away or say no to her. There was no getting out of this. At least ironing clothes wouldn't make any noise, and if it did, she would have been less vicious about it because I was doing her a favor. Not that she would have seen it that way. She must not have cared about the quality of the ironing if she was having a young boy do it for the first time. What did I know about ironing clothes? Yes, I'd seen it done—many times. Which wasn't helpful, though.

There is a method to ironing. You learn that as you go. I would iron the same garment, over and over, until I thought it was perfect. Then I would try to fold it, over and over, until I felt it perfectly folded. Then I tried doing it again on the next garment over and over until I got it perfect. The birth of my OCD?

Pants would get ironed with the inseams lined up together. Shirts would get ironed laid out flat on the ironing board. Fold everything to preserve the newly created creases. One by one, I removed the wrinkles born from the pile that the clothes had been left sitting in, in a basket fresh from the clothes dryer.

As I moved through the basket, I got the hang of this ironing thing. Iron the garment. Then perfectly fold the garment. Then stack it on the ironed clothes pile. I was thinking, I like this ironing thing. One piece at a time. One piece from start to finish. Then on to the next. Order. Structure. Repetition. I liked the repetition. It gave me familiarity. Security. It was my only stability in that nap-infested life of ours. My only comfort. I liked the idea of having accomplished something. Something that had a jumbled beginning and then a particularly good ending—a neat and orderly ending. An achievement. I've come to live my life always having some things accomplished before the end of each day. Maybe learning to iron did that for me.

The pile of clothes in the basket was getting smaller. The pile of clothes that were ironed, folded, and placed in the folded clothes pile was getting larger. I had created a tower of ironed and folded clothes. I felt disappointed as the task neared completion. I couldn't stop if life and all its noises had not yet resumed. Underwear. Underwear can be ironed. And I did so, one pair at a time. Meticulously. As ironing should be done. The only thing left in the basket were socks. I pulled out two matching socks. Socks can be ironed. I ironed one sock at a time. I folded the socks and placed them on my pile of ironed and folded garments. I pulled out another pair of matching socks. Iron, fold, and place.

My tower of ironed and folded clothes was a skyscraper. The larger garments on the bottom. The underwear and socks on the top. Sadly, my tower of neatly pressed and folded clothes gave me a sense of joy. I'll take that. There otherwise wasn't much joy with her napping my life away.

I iron clothes to this day. I usually dread getting to it. But, when I begin, it all comes back to me. One piece at a time. Neatly pressed. Properly folded. Wrinkled, then crisp. Start to finish. A sense of accomplishment. Joy.

Driftwood

My journey… a pathway over a lifetime of mistakes, regrets, joys, and jubilations. I've cared deeply for others. I've wiped away tears from many young faces, written encouraging notes to those in need, celebrated the accomplishments of unlikely achievers, provided guidance with humility, taught many, and learned much. I believe it is fitting that I write my interpretation of a journey shared by so many. The meditative healing power of just writing alone brings me peace. Line after line, that twist and turn. Lines that reveal a history beneath the soul's veil. It slows my thoughts and allows me to sink deeper into my mind. It is my calm in a world with unending stimuli and an unrelenting rush to live life.

No longer the mighty oak, I have been washed through the lakes and rivers of life, coursed through the sea of humanity, and smoothed by the tide and wind, bleached by salt and sun. Driftwood. Not yet the end of life, but now time to rest in a garden—tucked away in a compact green oasis, with the many plants blossoming around me while lost in my thoughts and memories, appreciated for any inspiration that I may bring. Like a cardinal in the snow. An ornament in a green haven, with multitudes of fragrant colors and stones of antiquity.

Each year passes, and who I might have been fades. A loss elusive and unnamed. A fleeting vision that I failed to make real. My old identity passed un-mourned. Once-hard edges take on a soft pale glow. The bright saturated colors of autumn fade into muddy earth tones, the smokey hues of dawn and dusk. Dry leaves that have fallen littering the ground. The residue of a life lived. Imperfect, yes. But lived.

The years have gone by, many of them without me, because of passions I chose not to pursue. Desires that have drifted but had my attention either way. My thoughts, insecurities, secrets, and unfulfilled passions will be buried with me. Passions quietly mine during a lifetime and still mine alone upon my death. Not a sadness to bear but a reality to accept.

I have a spiritual longing for a home that may never have existed. Nostalgia for an ancient place to which I cannot return or have never been. I think of it as the echo of a lost place in my soul's past and my grieving for it. It is the unnamable feelings of the Japanese philosophy of wabi-sabi: accepting the beauty of imperfection. It is the steady flicker inside me dimming in the darkening years of my life.

Throughout these twists and turns, my life has been an air of wreckage and ruins, with needs and disappointments, desires, conquests, and pleasures. But everything in this world is temporary and imperfect, so I invite peace into what is left of my days—to calm the storms, to quiet the mind, and to settle the spirit. Loss, once it becomes a certainty, is like a rock. It has weight, dimension, and texture. It is solid and can be assessed and dealt with. It can be a weapon of self-harm, or it can be tossed away. The condition of my end, the uncertainty of my death. I feel a sense of deep and mindless restlessness when I think of it. My most reliable reaction to the challenges of life as driftwood.

Other Than Among Us

As we journey into the schools of America, we will discover that we are looking at a societal rather than an educational problem. There is such a great combination of issues that you may realize that these kids are caught up in a community, a culture, and a system that all need fixing.

And you may start to recognize that these kids have no exit unless you change their family dynamics, their communities, and the culture they are caught up in. The adults in the system have prejudices, and while in a profession that should be absent from passing judgment, they bring their own, sometimes harmful, ideologies into it.

Ohanko was in a system not of his own making and could not easily exit that system. Looking back, the "then and now" excuse that we as adults rely upon to explain the guilt of past experiences is seldom satisfying. Sometimes life calls for deeper answers.

Hank—a simple, ordinary, unrevealing name. He was a newcomer to our junior high school community. We learned that he and his family would often relocate from one place to another. With some prodding from a few of us, he reluctantly described his home. His mother, aunt, grandmother, cousins, sister, and brother all lived together in the same household.

Although he was in our grade, he was bigger, so we presumed he was older. His dark skin cast a beautiful reddish undertone, accentuating his straight black hair and deep, almond-shaped, dark eyes. His round face bore a deep scar from his high cheekbone down to the corner of his mouth. Many of us had tragic experiences with our family demons, so we knew not to ask how he got it. That didn't mean we didn't talk about it when he wasn't around. Not knowing how he got the scar, we made up our own stories to explain it, and our imaginations ran wild, as was often the case with us.

He looked slightly different from the rest of us, and we soon learned that he was. In the isolated world of our neighborhood, and as youngsters, our social and cultural ethnocentrism was as strong and as vibrant as our many other youthful energies. Hank, as it turned out, was Native American—to us, an Indian. I don't believe we ever knew what tribe; I don't think we cared at the time. To us, an Indian was an Indian, and cultural or ethnic distinctions among them were either unknown to us or unimportant. He was the first authentic Indian we had ever met; first impressions are lasting impressions. He told us his real name was Ohanko, meaning Reckless, but the teachers always called him Hank.

Hank shared in our recreational activities—in the park by the cemetery, on the playground we called O'Connor's, and on the grounds of Roosevelt School—and he seemed to fit in well. But, as often as Hank was among us, he seemed elsewhere. He appeared distant, removed, far from where we all were. He was able to take part in our play and did so. But he was noticeably unenthused and mentally removed. Indifferent would describe Hank's general demeanor. We assumed he had family troubles or a difficult and tragic past, like many of us did, and that he shielded himself in our presence. We knew as kids that when one of us in the neighborhood was having family problems, we didn't ask about them. We all had them, and it was an unwritten rule among us that all the embarrassing family conflicts were off-limits to each other.

Whatever the reasons, Hank never laughed and never smiled. He didn't give the appearance of enjoying himself. He dutifully played among us as if following a script. Missing was that natural liveliness found in children, that youthful nature kids carry with them before life's experiences tear it away. His heart was missing from the joyful moments of play, likely from having a difficult and painful childhood, possibly tragic even, given his deep facial scar. Hank was good about going through the motions of play we expected from him. It satisfied us but appeared to leave him empty. If we could see this in him at our young age, then his demoralized temperament was clearly prominent.

Hank was with us for less than a school year, and he went away as quietly and uneventfully as when he first arrived. He gave no warning of his departure, and after weeks of being absent, we were informed that he and his family had, yet again, moved away. Our teacher, like many of the educators in our school at the time—elderly, white, Protestant women—told us that Hank was an Indian and that he and his family didn't belong. That same teacher had also made it clear that Tommy Ray, an African American boy among us, was not to attend religious instruction at our neighborhood Catholic church, a mistake I had made when I invited Tommy Ray to accompany me to our once-a-week religious instruction class.

Puzzling as these revelations were, we had accepted them, as they came from adults with authority—kids who were different had a place other than the one among us. If you look at our neighborhood gang, we were quite different from one another in so many ways. But none of us were Native American, and for that, we belonged in our community, so we were led to believe.

Hank left a lasting impression, and I wondered if I would ever see him again. His muted personality and listless spirit continue to perplex me. Perhaps it is clearer to me now why Hank was as Hank was, and why he came and went as he did. As heartbreaking as it was, Hank and his family needed to feel a sense of belonging somewhere safe and accepting. If a school community couldn't offer safety and acceptance for those considered different, then where would they get it? If only I knew then what I know now. And somehow, years later, I feel guilty that I didn't know, sorry that I couldn't help. Of course, that was then. Things have changed… or have they? Are there some among us now considered different who belong other than among us, according to today's adults representing authority? Sadly, it appears so.

It is the Pain That I Write

I write of pain—that which is mine and that of my loved ones. I write narratives out of life's most painful and tragic experiences. I write of the pain and anxiety of my childhood and young adult life. And I write of my lover's pain-ridden childhood and his young adult life. He is my whole world, the one that causes me to hate anyone or anything that has brought him harm or hurt.

I write because I know pain. Pain that has scarred me. Pain that should not be on the written page. I write of my broken-heartedness, physical and emotional abuse, and the abuse of those closest to me. I write of pain buried deep inside me. Pain that my memories hold. Pain that has scarred my humanity. Pain that should not have been experienced. Pain that was inflicted by those who were also scarred by pain.

Pain should not be easy to write about, but it is... easier than everything else. When I write of pain, I am reliving it and releasing it—my attempts at healing. Writing of pleasant and cheerful times is not yet possible for me. Writing anything that may be lighthearted or merry requires forgetting what is in my head and heart. To have a pleasant memory is to have a sensation, a yearning, for something that defies articulation. Pain cuts a deeper memory. It erases any significance to those events or experiences the mind may also hold. Memories aren't made. They simply occur. No, not simply. But brutally.

My writing lacks the uplifting details of time and place. There is no room for them when writing about pain. Was the sky sunny or gray? Not important, but likely gray. Were the leaves green, or had they fallen with winter? No matter, but likely have fallen. Was it a beautiful twilight night with all the stars shining, or was it black as the night should be? Probably as black as night should be. When writing about pain, those details are not important.

This pain has brought me to my knees on more than one occasion. It has caused me to believe that I need not be and need not continue. This pain has brought about the once-satisfying pleasure of knowing that I can cease to exist should I choose not to. And I have chosen not to, many times… or was it weakness?

But I am still here. The uncompromising touch of death has put a keener edge on my appreciation for life; that touch of death has come so often over the years. But now, I cannot cease to exist. I cannot be brought to my knees. I now know that it was then, a long time ago. That it is not now. But it is now that I can be aware of those painful memories and remain calm in my heart.

I've had to learn to dance in the storm, and I choose to dance. I have peace. I am aware of my inner turmoil and regret, but I have calm in that storm that will always be.

Yes, I have peace. So why does writing about the pain seem to be what I must do? I do what is necessary to convey what is essential to healing and to keep that peace and calm in my heart. I have found peace in the ones I love, those I do not wish to hurt, and the love of my life.

The love of my life... that proud and confident being who found his way into my heart; the love of my life... with all his wisdom, his kindness, and his affection; the one who makes me laugh, the only one who can make me cry, the one who has gifted me the desire to continue to exist.

Yes, the sky is sunny. The leaves are green, and the night is a beautiful twilight with all the stars shining. I am still here and most fortunate to be... still here.

Thank you for supporting LGBTQ+ organizations

A portion of the proceeds from sales of this book will be donated to the following LBGTQ+ organizations:

Point Foundation (LGBTQ students)
EIN # 84-1582086

The Trevor Project (LGBTQ students)
EIN # 95-4681287

SAGE Advocacy & Services for LGBTQ+ Elders
EIN # 13-2947657

Pride Center of the Capital Region, Albany, NY
EIN # 14-1605106

About the Author

Jack Cooper lives with his husband and Great Dane, Jack, in up-state New York, where he writes and renovates properties.

He has an MA from Union College, spent 20 years in the private sector, and taught at the secondary level for 25 years.

His work has been published in the Flumes Literary Journal, Weasel Press, Limit Experience Journal, Coffee People Zine, Miracle Monocle, Plentitudes Journal, Prometheus Dreaming, Two Sisters Writing and Publishing, Pride and Presents, Red Noise Collective, Running Wild Press Short Story Anthology, Wingless Dreamers Publication, Wild Sounds Writing Festival, Beyond Words, Beyond Queer Words, and RIZE Short Story Anthology.

You can contact him at
Jackcooperauthor@gmail.com.

Please review this book on Amazon.com

Please help my mission of getting this book into the hands and hearts of those who need it most, by posting a review on Amazon.com. Your comments and ratings will help elevate this book's visibility and ranking on Amazon.com, which helps more people discover it, read it, and share it.

I thank you in advance for your willingness to review this book on Amazon.com while it's fresh in your mind.

Endnotes

1 Klein, Adam. 2017. "Biomythography: Fact and Fiction as Identity."
  SUNY Geneseo English Department Nonfiction. https://nonfiction.su-
  nygeneseoenglish.org/2017/04/02/biomythography-fact-and-fiction-
  as-identity/.

2 Klein, Adam. 2017. "Biomythography: Fact and Fiction as Identity."
  SUNY Geneseo English Department Nonfiction. https://nonfiction.su-
  nygeneseoenglish.org/2017/04/02/biomythography-fact-and-fiction-
  as-identity/.

3 *Fear in Utica: Who Killed David Gray?* Sullivan County Demo-
  crat. February 1, 1976. https://www.nyshistoricnewspapers.
  org/?a=d&d=snt19760201-01.1.8&e=-------en-20--1--txt-tx-
  IN----------

www.ingramcontent.com/pod-product-compliance
Lightning Source LLC
Chambersburg PA
CBHW031752200726

48289CB00013B/792